### "I'll be fine. You don't need to worry."

He nodded. "Just to make sure, I'll leave Decoy with you. He didn't do all that well with those attack commands, but he's still big enough to scare someone off."

Piper hoped she wouldn't need to use any attack commands, but just in case...

"Thank you. I'll take good care of him," she said and rubbed Decoy's ears. The dog sidled up to her, happy for the attention. "Good boy."

"I know you will, but...take good care of yourself as well. I'll see you in the morning," he said and took a step back into the alcove by her front door. He gestured to the alarm pad and said, "Lock up and set that thing."

"Thanks," she said. Then she quickly added, "We can start training again in the morning."

Her words lightened his features and a smile skipped across his lips. "I'd like that."

"I would, too," she said and quickly closed the door.

To my daughter Samantha and her amazing creativity! Thank you for dragging me into TikTok and for being my best PR person. I am so proud of *Seoul Searching* and all the exciting things you're doing with Korean from Context. Saranghae, ttal.

# DECOY TRAINING

---

**New York Times Bestselling Author**
## CARIDAD PIÑEIRO

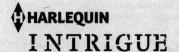

**HARLEQUIN**
INTRIGUE

Special thanks and acknowledgment are given to Caridad Piñeiro for her contribution to the K-9s on Patrol miniseries.

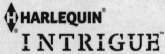

**HARLEQUIN®**
**INTRIGUE™**

Recycling programs for this product may not exist in your area.

ISBN-13: 978-1-335-48950-0

Decoy Training

Copyright © 2022 by Harlequin Books S.A.

This edition published by arrangement with Harlequin Books S.A.

For questions and comments about the quality of this book, please contact us at CustomerService@Harlequin.com.

Harlequin Enterprises ULC
22 Adelaide St. West, 41st Floor
Toronto, Ontario M5H 4E3, Canada
www.Harlequin.com

**Printed in U.S.A.**

*New York Times* and *USA TODAY* bestselling author **Caridad Piñeiro** is a Jersey girl who just wants to write and is the author of nearly fifty novels and novellas. She loves romance novels, superheroes, TV and cooking. For more information on Caridad and her dark, sexy romantic suspense and paranormal romances, please visit www.caridad.com.

**Books by Caridad Piñeiro**

**Harlequin Intrigue**

*Cold Case Reopened*
*Trapping a Terrorist*
*Decoy Training*

Visit the Author Profile page at Harlequin.com.

# CAST OF CHARACTERS

*Shane Adler*—Army veteran Shane Adler knows no life besides the military, and when an injury forces Shane to retire, he's lost. When a friend suggests that the dog who saved him from the rubble of a car bomb might make a good search and rescue candidate, Shane heads to the Daniels Canine Academy in Idaho to try to find what he's meant to do with his new and unexpected life.

*Piper Lambert*—After the death of her marine husband four years earlier, Piper was inconsolable. With the help of her best friend, Emma Daniels, Piper has managed to rebuild her life and find satisfaction as an instructor at the Daniels Canine Academy.

*Emma Daniels*—When her foster father and mother passed, Emma decided to honor them by turning their ranch into the Daniels Canine Academy and by fostering other at-risk children the way the Danielses had saved her as a child.

*Tashya Pratt*—Tashya is one of the children whom Emma Daniels helped foster. With Emma's help, Tashya was able to attend vet tech school in Boise, and now that she's finished, Tashya is back to help Emma at the Daniels Canine Academy.

*Ava Callan*—Police officer Ava Callan desperately needed a change of scenery and left her job in Chicago to join the police force in a small Idaho town. Ava is having a tough time dealing with the change. Her chief has her training at the Daniels Canine Academy in the hopes that she will acclimate to her new town and forge relationships with Piper and Emma as well as the other officers on the force.

*Brady Nichols*—Jasper police officer Brady Nichols has been partnering with Ava Callan. Brady trained his K-9 partner at the Daniels Canine Academy and is a regular visitor to the DCA.

# Chapter One

The "Welcome to California" sign mocked him as it became increasingly smaller in his side-view mirror.

Shane Adler shot a quick look at the Lab/hound mix sitting in the bucket chair of his pickup. "What do you think about leaving Cali, Decoy? Are you excited, boy?"

Decoy looked at Shane and cocked his head, his brown-eyed gaze almost human. Questioning.

"Yeah, I'm not sure either, but what the heck," he said and wondered if he was losing it by treating the dog as if he were human. But Decoy had been his constant companion since arriving in the States a few weeks ago from Afghanistan. He had befriended the stray pup while on assignment, feeding it scraps and letting it follow him around while he trained his fellow soldiers. They had become inseparable after Decoy had found him in the rubble left by the explosion of a car bomb.

Shane reached out to rub the dog's head, but his shoulder painfully spasmed, making his hand shake violently, courtesy of the shrapnel from the blast, which had damaged his shoulder and ended his career as an Army sharpshooter trainer.

Upon his return to his home base at the Fort Irwin National Training Center, Shane had been at loose ends, and staying near the center only brought daily reminders of what he could no longer be: a soldier. It had been his dream since he'd been a little child and now that dream was done.

Deciding he needed a change of scenery, he'd packed up his things and bought an RV to transport him from his old life in the Army to somewhere else.

Anywhere else.

First stop: Boise, Idaho. In a little over twelve hours and nearly eight hundred miles, he'd visit an old Army pal who'd been honorably discharged a couple of years earlier. Shane hoped that with some time and distance from California, he could decide what he and Decoy would do with the rest of their lives.

The open road stretched out ahead of him, the white stripes on the black asphalt and sound of the wheels on the pavement creating an almost lulling rhythm. Between much-needed coffee and bathroom breaks, they didn't arrive in Boise until dusk was settling over the area.

He had no sooner parked his pickup and the RV on the street when his friend threw open the door of his home and wheeled down a wooden ramp to greet him.

He slipped out of the pickup, bent to bro-hug his friend and gripped his hand tightly. When he straightened, Shane said, "You're looking great, Gonzo." His friend appeared fit with thicker muscle across his upper body, but more importantly, his whole attitude was relaxed. There was a happy gleam in his green-eyed gaze that relieved Shane of worry about how his friend was doing.

"Feeling great, Shane. You're looking a little…tired," Gonzo said, never one to mince words. As Decoy sidled next to Gonzo, he rubbed the gold-brown fur around the dog's floppy ears. "Who's your little friend?"

"Name's Decoy. Saved my butt in Afghanistan so I couldn't leave him behind," Shane said and glanced at the dog, who barked and wagged his head as if to agree.

"No man or dog left behind," Gonzo said with a broad smile, then executed a perfect 180 and wheeled himself back up the ramp.

Shane and Decoy followed him into the modest ranch home, and once inside, Gonzo spread his arms wide. "Welcome to my home. *Mi casa es su casa.*"

"*Gracias, amigo.* I appreciate you letting me chill with you for a little bit," Shane said, his tone heartfelt. He and Gonzo, Gonzalo to his Lopez family members, had been teammates until the bullet that had nearly taken Gonzo's life had stolen his legs and Army career.

"My pleasure. My *mami* is looking forward to seeing you, too," Gonzo said and gestured to a nearby sofa.

"Please don't tell me your mom is already matchmaking," Shane said as he sat and Decoy circled around a couple of times before settling at his feet, head tucked onto his large paws.

Gonzo held his hands up as if in surrender. "I told her that you're just here for a few days, but you know *Mami.*"

Shane did. Every time that they'd gotten together here in Boise, Gonzo's mom had tried to find a girlfriend for Shane, hoping he'd settle down. Only Shane hadn't been sure back then and he was even more un-sure now about what his future might entail. Changing the subject, he said, "How are *you* doing?"

Gonzo shrugged. "Dealing, *mano*. Getting strong," Gonzo said and flexed the hard muscles of his arms. "I've also been volunteering with a group that helps troubled teens. Demanding, but I understand them. The first few months after this were really hard to accept," he said and slapped the arms of the wheelchair.

"I wish I could have been here for you," Shane said, but he'd been deployed and unable to visit his friend until his short breaks between missions.

"You helped more than you know. I hope I can do the same, *mano*. How's the shoulder?"

Shane did a little roll with his injured arm and held his hand out. Only a small tremble, but it was enough to make it impossible to handle a weapon precisely. "Working. Not much pain, but some moves are hard," he said. It was the other things, like nightmares about the explosion and being trapped beneath the debris, that still rattled him more often than he liked. But he wasn't ready to share that with anyone, even a good buddy like Gonzo.

Gonzo narrowed his gaze, clearly assessing him. "Calling you out on that, but not going to push 'cuz I know how hardheaded you can be. Are you hungry?"

In answer, his stomach rumbled, and he splayed his hand there to quiet it. "Starving. I'm hoping your mom loves me enough to have made her world-famous tama-les," he said, optimistic.

Gonzo's smile was easygoing and lit up his green eyes with happiness. "She did. I just have to crank up the steam to warm them. How about a beer while we wait?"

"I'd love one," he said and followed Gonzo to the kitchen, where he noted how the space had been adapted to make it more accessible for his friend. Counters had been dropped for easier reach and were free of any lower cabinets in many sections, allowing Gonzo to slip his wheelchair beneath to work. The upper cabinets were open-shelf mechanisms that pulled down for access.

"This is cool, bro," Shane said as he looked around the kitchen, which had been remodeled since his last visit.

"It's made my life easier, but my girlfriend finds it a little challenging," he said as he took a pot and placed it on a cooktop whose height had also been adapted.

"Girlfriend? Is it serious?" Shane asked, surprised because Gonzo had always been a player before his injury.

His friend's shrug provided an answer, but also questions. "I guess it is serious," Shane said and got another awkward shrug.

"It's tough, with me being like this and all, but she's amazing. I'm a lucky man," Gonzo said as he turned the heat up under the pot with the tamales.

Shane clapped his friend on the back. "If she's amazing, don't lose her, bro."

Gonzo shot him a look over his shoulder, a broad smile on his face. "I won't, but that's funny advice coming from you."

Shane dipped his head in acknowledgment. "It is," he said because he couldn't disagree. He had no clue about lasting relationships, so telling his buddy what to do was…ironic.

But he kept silent as the two of them worked in the kitchen to finish preparing the meal and set the table. While they ate, they shared beers and chatted about how Gonzo's mother was doing, his girlfriend and his work with the troubled teens.

As he had before, Decoy took a spot at Shane's feet and Gonzo didn't fail to notice. "You guys *are* insepa-rable."

Shane nodded and glanced down at his dog, whose gaze perked up with the attention. "We are. I owe him big-time," he said and offered Decoy a treat from the table. Decoy eagerly snapped up the piece of tamale and sat up, anxiously awaiting another bite.

Gonzo delayed for a moment and then said, "Some of my troubled teens spend time at a dog training facil-ity. It helps them learn discipline by taking care of the dogs and doing chores in the kennels and barn."

"Sounds like it works for them," Shane said and forked up another piece of tamale, enjoying the tasty mix of the sweet corn masa and flavorful pork.

"It does. I'm impressed by how much they change after only a few weeks, but you know, Decoy looks like a Lab/hound mix and might be great at something like search and rescue. I mean, he saved you, right?" Gonzo said and gestured to Decoy with his beer bottle.

Shane glanced down at the dog, who peered up at him with love and trust. Much like Decoy had saved his life, he had rescued Decoy and maybe that had been for a reason, he thought, intrigued by Gonzo's idea.

"He is a smart dog and great at finding things,"

Shane said, thinking about how much Decoy loved it when they played hide-and-seek and how he'd found Shane in the wreck of what had once been their training building.

"What's the name of this place?" he asked.

"Daniels Canine Academy. I know the owner. Emma Daniels. You interested?" Gonzo said, although he suspected his friend already knew what the answer would be.

"Yes, I am. Can you make the connection?"

"I'd love to, *mano*. Here's to new beginnings," Gonzo said and raised his beer bottle as if in a toast.

Shane wasn't quite sure it was a new beginning, but it was definitely something worth exploring, he thought, and clinked his beer bottle against Gonzo's.

PIPER LAMBERT SAT beside her best friend, Emma Daniels, as the two of them listened to the Jasper police chief explain about their newest recruit, Ava Callan.

"Ava is a good cop. We're lucky to have snagged her from Chicago PD. She's got great skills, but I think she's having a little trouble fitting in with all the men and small-town life in Jasper," Chief Walters said. He was a sixty-something man with broad shoulders and thick muscle that was starting to go soft around his midsection. His brown-eyed gaze was warm and caring as it settled on Emma and he said, "I know you understand, Em."

"I do, Chief," Emma said. The chief had been the man who had taken Emma under his wing after her adoptive father, a K-9 police officer, had died in the line of duty and Emma had lost her way.

Much like Piper had lost her way when her Marine sergeant husband had been killed in Iraq four years earlier. Luckily, Emma had offered her home and her business as a way to rebuild her life. *So far things are going well,* she thought. She'd learned so much to become a dog trainer and loved sharing that knowledge with others.

"I think that pairing Ava with a dog and working with the two of you will help her develop a sense of belonging on the force and in town," he said and ran a hand through his receding gray hair.

"We'd be happy to have her with us, Chief. Let us know when she's coming and Piper and I will pick a dog for her so we can start her training," Emma said.

Chief Walters smiled and slowly got to his feet, grimacing a little as he did so.

"You okay, Chief?" Piper asked.

The older man smiled and nodded. "Just a touch of arthritis" he said playfully, but she and Emma knew the chief was counting down to when he would retire and ride off into the sunset to fly-fish with his retired K-9 partner, Buddy, who had been peacefully resting at the chief's feet during their meeting in Emma's living room. Emma normally met with clients in her office, but the chief was family.

Emma slipped her arm through the older man's, who was almost like a second dad to her. "It was nice seeing you today, even if it was for work. Hopefully you'll come around more often when you retire."

"Count on it, Emma. I love seeing what you're doing here and I'm so proud of you," he said and hugged her before facing Piper.

"You, too, Piper. You've been doing some amazing things with the K-9s for our department," he said and left Emma's side to embrace her.

"It's my pleasure, Chief. It's great to work with everyone on the force," she said, but the older man saw through her words.

"Except Captain Rutledge," he said as they strolled out of Emma's house and to the large driveway area where the police chief had parked his white Durango. The police force's emblem, a shield honoring the area's mountains, woods and the nearby Salmon River, was emblazoned on the door, his badge and a patch on the sleeve of his black uniform shirt.

"Except Captain Rutledge," Emma repeated. "It's obvious he's not a fan of the K-9 partners you've added to the force."

Chief Walters paused by the vehicle, arms akimbo. "Rutledge is an issue, and not just because of the K-9s. I keep on hoping he'll learn to play well with others, but…"

He didn't need to finish since both she and Emma were aware of the issues the chief had with his second-in-command and the other officers in the department.

"It'll work out," Piper said, hoping that no matter what happened when the chief retired, it would not impact the business her friend had worked so hard to build.

"It will," Emma said with a bob of her head as they watched the chief get into his SUV and drive away. After, Emma slipped her arm through Piper's, and with a tug, led her toward the facility that held the offices for the DCA, a small indoor training room, runs for the dogs and climate-controlled kennels.

"Did I mention we have a new client? Gonzo recommended him to us," Emma said and tilted her head to glance at Piper. Strands of sun-streaked light brown hair had escaped the ponytail Emma usually wore, and her blue-eyed gaze sparkled with joy.

"Any friend of Gonzo's is a friend of ours," she said. The Army vet's program with troubled teens had been a success and when combined with Emma's program for local at-risk teens, like the three young men currently at work in the kennels and barn, she felt like she was making a real difference in people's lives.

"Great. I was hoping you'd work with him and his dog. It's a Lab/hound mix and he's thinking they might go on to work with a search and rescue group," Emma said.

"Labs and hounds are wonderful for SAR, so hopefully his dog will be good for that," Piper said, remembering some of their clients with similar animals who had gone on to do search and rescue in various groups throughout the country.

"I hope so, too. He's just left the Army and he sounded… I'm not sure what to call it," Emma said as they walked into her office, where she snared a manila folder from her desktop.

*Military. Great,* Piper thought. She had nothing but the utmost respect for those who served and their families, but she had her own issues because sometimes military men reminded her way too much of her dead husband. Those were memories she'd rather keep buried to avoid the pain they brought.

Piper took the file for their new client and opened it, but barely skimmed through the paperwork before handing it back to her friend. "Are you sure I'm the right trainer for him?"

Emma arched a brow. "Positive, Piper. You know, sometimes a trainer can learn things as well when they're working with a client."

She knew she wasn't perfect, far from it, but as for what she needed to learn…

"I'll do my best," she said and shot a quick glance at her smartphone as it vibrated to remind her of an upcoming meeting.

"Something wrong?" Emma asked, eyes narrowed as she glanced at her.

Piper held up her phone. "Just a reminder to see Tashya about the puppies that Jasper PD found last week. I was thinking of maybe picking one for myself."

"Good to hear. You've wanted your own dog for a long time," Emma said and clapped her hands happily.

"I have and those cute puppies Macon brought over may be perfect," she said, and didn't fail to notice the little wince at the mention of Emma's former client before her friend schooled her emotions. It had been clear to everyone that there had been a spark between Macon and Emma when he had been training with them.

"They may be," she said and gestured to her desk. "I've got a few calls to make before I quit for the day. Feel like meeting me at Millard's Diner for dinner?"

"I never say no to one of their burgers," Piper said, but thought it funny that Emma would choose a spot that was a hangout for the local police officers, including Macon Ridley. But the diner was a fun place to eat with red vinyl booths, bright blue counters and even a jukebox that gave it a very retro '50s vibe.

"Six sound good?"

"Six is perfect," she said and rushed out to meet Tashya, the young vet tech who had been one of many foster children Emma had taken in over the years, much like the Danielses had fostered Emma after she was removed from a home plagued by domestic violence. Thanks to the life insurance money left to her by her foster mom, Emma had been able to turn the Daniels homestead into the DCA and had fostered a number of children over the years to honor her adoptive parents.

As she neared one of the kennels, she heard Tashya's playful laughter, and it brightened the pall cast over her by the prospect of having to work with her new client.

Shane Adler. Ex-Army sharpshooter and instructor. Wounded vet.

A dangerous mix for a variety of reasons.

But at the sight of Tashya laughing and surrounded by over half a dozen playful pups that jumped up and climbed all over her, her worries fell away.

When she entered the kennel, one little dog bounded away from Tashya and sauntered over to her, a jaunty smile on her white-and-tan face. The puppies were a corgi/pit mix and would need little grooming thanks to their short hair, but a lot of attention since pits could be needy and very active.

She scooped up the pup, who wriggled in her arms and licked doggy kisses all along her jaw. "Easy, girl. I love you, too," she said with a laugh, but didn't release her as she walked to Tashya.

"That one is a handful," the young vet tech said as she finished examining the last puppy and shot to her feet.

"Is she ready to be adopted?" Piper asked, eager to start training the little dog.

"Dr. Beaumont said you can take her home tomorrow after the last of her shots."

"How is Marie doing?" Piper said. She hadn't seen the vet in weeks since she'd been so wrapped up with work at the DCA.

"She's busy. Her vet business is doing well. Any idea what you'll name your pup?" Tashya asked as she rubbed the puppy's head.

Piper peered at the little dog, and the pup immediately gave Piper her attention. With her perpetual corgi smile, she radiated cheer, which prompted Piper to say, "Chipper." The dog yipped, almost as if approving of Piper's choice.

Tashya threw her head back in laughter, her smile bright against the creamy brown of her skin. "I'll round up what you'll need to take her home."

"Thank you so much. I'll come by after work tomorrow," she said and hugged the young woman before heading home.

She walked away into the gap between the barn where Emma kept two rescue horses and the building that held their offices and kennels. Behind the buildings was an open gap in the surrounding tree line and a small path through a nearby meadow to her tidy ranch house. She and Emma had worn down that path with the many times they'd used it. It was barely a ten-minute walk and when the weather was nice, as it was today despite a slight April chill, she loved to do the hike to stretch her legs and appreciate the beauty of the nature around them, especially since in the winter three or four feet of snow might blanket the ground, making the trek difficult unless she hauled out her cross-country skis. Emma often did the walk over to Piper's house as well for a girls' night.

The ground was a little soft from an earlier rain and the air still had that rain-fresh smell tinged with the scent of pines and fir from the nearby evergreens. The first spring wildflowers were beginning to blossom, painting the ground with shades of yellow, purple and white. After the April rains, the meadows would burst to life with the white and pink of woodland stars, purples of clematis and shooting stars, and the bright yellows of arrowleaf balsamroot and heartleaf arnica.

In the distance, the mountains rose up, snow frosting the highest peaks, but most of the snow would melt in the next few weeks and the flowers would start to blossom at those higher elevations.

But today the beauty of the nature around her didn't bring as much calm as it usually did, maybe because she had a niggling sense something wasn't right as she neared the backyard of her home.

Piper looked around, searching for the source of that disquiet, but didn't see anything when she walked to the front door. A weird feeling came to her, as if she was being watched, only after another quick look around, she didn't see anyone or anything, like the occasional black bear that sometimes wandered out of the woods. Then a smell wafted to her: cigarette smoke. Only there was no other home around for at least a couple of hundred feet.

Hands on her hips, she did a slow pivot once again,

searching for the source of the odor, but couldn't find a thing.

*Maybe I'm imagining it, or the smell came from a passing car,* she thought, but that feeling of being watched chased her into her home, making her feel uneasy until she closed the door behind her and double-locked it. Only then did she feel relief.

She hoped that relief would last with the arrival of their new client.

Shane Adler. From the brief look she had gotten at his paperwork in the file Emma had passed to her, she knew he was a wounded vet and bound to have his demons, but so did she.

Maybe together they could find a way to exorcise those demons and move on with their lives.

## Chapter Two

Shane stood by the firepit and stared at the Salmon River as it wound past the campground where he'd parked his RV. The air was frosty and scented with the fresh fragrance from a nearby stand of pines and the smoky remnants of last night's fire. Decoy sprawled beside him on the rug he had spread out on the smooth stones all around the living area for his camping space.

He'd arrived in the early morning the day before, eager to get settled before his first day at the Daniels Canine Academy. It had been a short drive from Gonzo's in Boise, just over three hours. That had given him time to stop in Jasper for groceries and other supplies.

The town was the kind of peaceful and picturesque small town that 1950s Hollywood would adore. Quaint shops, restaurants and well-kept older homes lined one side of Main Street and led to a central park with a gazebo. A vet's office, the fire and police departments and town hall were at the west side of the square. A library, shops and professional offices surrounded the park while the west end of Main Street led in the direction of the Salmon River and his campground.

*After the chaos of life as a soldier, Jasper might be*

*just what I need,* Shane thought and with a low whistle at Decoy, headed to his pickup for the drive to the training center. The DCA was only twenty minutes away, but he didn't want to be late.

His parents had always told him that being late was a sign of disrespect and the military had only reinforced the importance of timeliness.

As he drove, he took note of the older but nicely maintained homes on large-sized properties along the road. A newer gray and stone ranch home sat at the corner where his GPS told him to turn for the final half-mile drive to the DCA.

He stopped in the driveway where two large poles held up a wooden sign that read Daniels Canine Academy next to the silhouette of a German shepherd. Beyond the sign was a long driveway leading to a trio of buildings.

"What do you think, Decoy? Looks good, right?" he asked and shot a quick peek at his dog as Decoy sat in the passenger seat.

The dog cocked his head to the side and peered at Shane, but then Decoy surprised him with a quick bark as if to say, "Get a move on."

"Sure thing, boss," he said with a laugh and wheeled his pickup down the drive to the parking spaces opposite a rambling, green-roofed ranch house. When he exited his vehicle and leashed Decoy, he noticed the three women working with a litter of puppies in a fenced-in area in front of a large agility course.

He approached quietly, not wanting to interrupt the training, but also wanting to get a feel for the women.

Two of the women seemed to be of a similar age, late twenties if he had to guess.

The third was clearly younger, with a round baby face, beautiful light brown eyes and brown hair. She had a puppy on a leash and was watching as the other women played with a litter of short-legged, long-bodied dogs, but also worked basic commands into the play.

The taller of the women had a strong athletic build and sun-streaked light brown hair pulled back in a ponytail. She scooped up one of the playful puppies to observe the other woman as she worked with another little dog.

"Sit, Chipper," the second woman said with authority and combined it with a hand gesture. When the pup didn't immediately respond, she repeated the command and gently urged the pup's butt onto the ground. This time the command seemed to take, and she rewarded the little dog with a treat, squatted to rub its head and said, "Good girl, Chipper."

He couldn't avoid admiring her as she rose and raked back her long red hair with her fingers. As the puppy yipped at her, she tossed her head back and laughed, the sound pure and unfiltered.

It dragged a laugh from him and snared the attention of the three women.

The redhead went from joy to a chill as frosty as the snow on the nearby mountains, making him wonder about her abrupt change of mood.

"You must be Shane. Emma Daniels," said the one woman and walked over to shake his hand.

"Shane Adler. I'm looking forward to working with you," he said and from the corner of his eye he noticed as the redhead slowly approached where he stood at the fence railing.

"Actually, you'll be working with Piper," Emma said and tilted her head in the direction of the other woman who finally, reluctantly, held out her hand.

PIPER THOUGHT SHE'D be prepared for when she'd meet her new client, but she was totally wrong.

He was dangerously handsome, with broad shoulders and washboard abs that were visible beneath the cotton of his tight T-shirt. The soft denim of his jeans hugged long muscular legs. Intense blue eyes were framed by thick lashes any woman would wish for. A light stubble on his strong jaw and cheeks had hints of gray like those in the longer strands of hair at the top of his head.

He had been leaning on the railing and straightened to well over six feet as he said, "Shane Adler. Nice to meet you, Piper."

As he wrapped his big, calloused hand around hers, her gut clenched with awareness of his strength and masculinity. His blue eyes widened a bit before he reined in whatever emotion that had been and released her hand.

"Nice to meet you as well," she said, forcing positivity into her tone and hoping it didn't sound as artificial as it was.

The awkward exchange was luckily interrupted by the sharp yip of her puppy, Chipper, who had sneaked under the fence and was climbing all over Decoy. The older dog was calm, his head cocked almost indulgently as the puppy yapped and hopped on him, demanding attention.

"Chipper. Sit," Piper said and held up her palm in a hand signal. Surprisingly, the little pup responded, earning a treat and rub of her head to reinforce the training. "Good girl."

"She's a fast learner," said the younger woman with a laugh and held out her hand. "I'm Tashya Pratt, the DCA's vet tech."

"Nice to meet you, Tashya," he said and shook her hand.

When Chipper barked again and hopped up on his leg, Shane said, "I see you, girl. Now sit."

Chipper sat and Shane smiled and laughed as he bent to pat the little dog's head as her reward for the behavior and likewise rubbed Decoy's head to acknowledge his calm.

*That smile should be registered as a dangerous weapon*, Piper thought, unable to ignore how the smile and laughter totally transformed a face that had been hard as stone only seconds before making it look almost boyish.

That hard-as-stone visage was all too familiar to her. She'd seen it on her husband's face more than once, and sadly, their time of laughter and smiles had been cut short with his death.

As Shane straightened, that hardness slipped back into place, and she told herself that was for the best.

"Are you ready to get started?" she asked, picked up Chipper and handed her to Tashya, who would care for her until Piper took her home later that day.

"I'm ready if you are," he said with an arch of a dark brow, almost in challenge.

"Great," she said even though she wasn't ready in

any way, shape or form. "Let me show you around the place so you get familiar with it," she said and slipped beneath the fence railing to join him.

"I'D LIKE THAT. THANKS," Shane said and trailed after her as she walked him toward the two buildings beside the outdoor training ring. The closest building had a concrete base and dark wood above and was a nice-sized structure. Piper gestured to it and, as she opened the door, said, "This is really the heart of DCA."

He followed her into the building and to the first office where a forty-something woman with medium brown hair and light hazel eyes sat at a desk. The woman looked up and smiled as she saw them. She popped out of her chair and cheerfully introduced herself, "Barbara Macy. I'm Emma's assistant."

Shane shook her hand and smiled. "Shane Adler. Nice to meet you."

"Don't let her kid you. Barbara is more than just Emma's assistant. She's the Master of All and if you need anything, absolutely anything, Barbara is the person to see," Piper said with a laugh.

Barbara grinned and did a little curtsy. "Thank you so much, Piper."

They walked just a few feet and Piper said, "This is Emma's office, but it's probably easier to find her anywhere the dogs are training."

Sure enough, as they turned to walk back out, he caught sight of Emma and Tashya. They had moved to an indoor training area right by the offices and were working with the puppies once again. Although he couldn't call what they were doing training since some of the pups were busy playing with toys while others were starting to drop off for naps.

Piper must have sensed his confusion since she said, "It's important to let puppies play as part of their training and the toys can serve as positive reinforcement as good as any treat. We also move them to different environments so they're not afraid of other surroundings."

"Good to know," he said, thinking about how Decoy seemed to be confident no matter his location, maybe as a result of all the different areas he'd been exposed to in his short life. Including the rescue foundation's kennel in Afghanistan where he'd been kept while he and the foundation cut through all the red tape to get Decoy sent to the States.

They exited and walked past doors for a climate-controlled kennel area and then large outside dog runs.

"As you can see, we have plenty of room for the dogs to stay with us and also have a place to be outside."

"Do you keep a lot of animals with you?" he asked, impressed with the facilities and how well-maintained they appeared.

Piper stopped by one dog run to rub the head of a German shepherd who lapped up the attention. "That's a good dog, Lacey," she said, but then added, "Most trainees keep their dogs with them, but we sometimes have up to half a dozen dogs. We select some for training from nearby animal shelters while others are left by their owners for instruction. Occasionally we end up with rescues like those corgi/pit puppies."

When Piper rose, she gestured to the furthermost building, which was wooden and white and had a paddock next to it. A brown quarter horse and a black-

and-white-spotted Appaloosa were close to the wooden fence, nibbling at the grass along the edges. A large orange tabby sauntered out of the barn and walked toward the horses, who ignored the pudgy feline.

"That cat is Gus. You can pet him, but he'll flay you alive if you pick him up. He's a great rodent-catcher," she said with a shake of her head.

Shane laughed. "I can tell from that belly he's good at his job."

Piper joined in his laughter. The sound was musical, bright, and it once again lightened something inside him.

He didn't have time to let that sink in since Decoy suddenly barked and lunged toward the tabby, scaring it away.

"Sit, boy. Sit," he said, but Decoy tugged at the leash again until Piper grabbed hold of it and brought him tight to Shane's side and issued a strongly worded, "Sit."

The dog sat and peered up at Piper, apparently aware she wouldn't take any guff.

She bent slightly, rubbed the dog's ears and reached into her pocket to give him a treat. "Good boy, Decoy. Good boy."

"He's usually pretty obedient, but he's still learning," Shane said and likewise stroked Decoy's head.

Piper nodded and straightened again. "How long have you had him?"

It should have been an easy question to answer, and yet it wasn't. "Decoy's been with me several weeks now in the States, and before that, we were together in Afghanistan for about four or five months. I was deployed there as an Army sharpshooter trainer and Decoy was always hanging around our complex. I started feeding him and he kept on coming back."

He didn't fail to see the change that came over Piper at the mention of his military service. Every muscle in her body tensed and a dark cloud chased away the lightness that had been in her laughter just seconds before. He should have left it alone, but he couldn't. Especially if they were going to be working together for the next month.

"Something wrong?"

A stilted shrug followed before she wrapped her arms around herself in a defensive gesture he recognized all too well. He did it whenever anyone delved too deeply into why he was no longer a soldier.

Despite her obvious reticence, something made him push. "Well?"

He was challenging her already and they hadn't even really started working together, but if they were going to survive several weeks of training, honesty was going to be the best policy.

"My husband was a Marine," Piper said, but didn't make eye contact with him. Instead, she whirled and started walking back in the direction of the outdoor training ring.

He turned and kept pace beside her, his gaze trained on her face. "Was?"

Challenging again. Pushing, but regardless of that, she said, "He was killed in action in Iraq. Four years ago and yet…"

Her throat choked up and tears welled in her eyes as

she rushed forward, almost as if she could outrun the discussion and the pain it brought.

The gentle touch of his big, calloused hand on her forearm stopped her escape.

She glanced down at that hand and then followed his arm up to meet his gaze, so full of concern and something else. *Pain?*

"I'm sorry. It can't be easy," he said, the simple words filled with so much more. Pain for sure. Understanding. Compassion. Not pity, thankfully. The last nearly undid her, but she sucked in a breath, held it for the briefest second before blurting out, "We should get going. If you're going to do search and rescue with Decoy, we'll have to improve his obedience skills."

Rushing away from him, she slipped through the gaps in the split rail fence and walked to the center of the training ring.

Shane hesitated, obviously uneasy, but then he bent to go across the fence railing and met her in the middle of the ring, Decoy at his side.

"I'm ready if you are," he said, his big body several feet away only he still felt too close. Too big. Too masculine with that kind of posture and strength that screamed military.

She took a step back and said, "I'm ready."

She wasn't and didn't know if she ever could be with this man. He was testing her on too many levels.

Only she'd never failed a training assignment and she didn't intend to start with Shane and Decoy.

"Let's get going," she said.

## Chapter Three

Shane was pleased with how the afternoon had gone, especially considering the awkwardness when they had first begun their training.

That had ebbed little by little as Piper worked with them to determine how well Decoy responded to basic commands. Piper also instructed him on leash control and how to train Decoy to understand hand commands as well as verbal ones. In a search and rescue situation, it might not be possible to use verbal instructions, so Decoy would need to understand what to do with the hand signals.

By the end of the training session, Decoy had nailed both the verbal and hand commands for "Sit" and had started to understand "Look at me."

"That's a good boy," Piper said as she offered Decoy a treat and ruffled his golden-brown fur affectionately.

The dog rewarded her with sloppy dog kisses, yanking that bright almost musical laugh from her again.

She was beautiful when she laughed. It made her emerald gaze glitter and reminded him of the evergreens surrounding the area and blanketing the mountains in the distance.

As her gaze connected with his, he reined in his reaction and said, "I think it was a good day."

Piper nodded. "I think so, too. Decoy is a smart boy. Aren't you?"

The dog almost preened, raising his head to look at Piper and doing a quick little bark.

"He's a natural. I guess that's why he was able to find me," he said, then winced and braced himself for what the next question would be and how Piper would react.

"Labs and hounds love playing hide-and-seek. That's something we can work on as well," she said, but her tone was forced since she was clearly in avoidance mode as he was.

"Great," he said, his tone sharp.

She stiltedly repeated, "Great." She clapped her hands, wrapped her arms around herself, and said, "I think we should call it a day. Just remember to reinforce what he's learning with the leash control and treats."

"Will do." He walked with Piper out of the ring.

As they neared the kennel, Piper said, "Barbara mentioned to me earlier this morning that she needs you to fill out some additional forms."

"Okay. I'll go see her. I guess I'll see you tomorrow," he said, his tone filled with question.

"Tomorrow," she confirmed and hurried away into the gap between the two buildings.

PIPER COULDN'T GET away from Shane fast enough.

He challenged her on so many levels and she wasn't sure she was up for it.

There was the whole ex-Army thing that roused too many memories of her dead husband, David, although

Shane was nothing like David physically. David had been a blond, California-surfer-dude type with a lean build and average height. Handsome with his boyish grin whose memory even now brought lightness to her heart despite his loss.

Shane was all man and anything but boyish. His stubble and short-cropped hair were painted with the first strokes of gray. His blue-eyed gaze was intense and seemingly missed nothing based on how he had noticed the emotions she had thought she successfully hid from him and others.

And he was big, well over six feet with thick work-hardened muscle. Imposing.

It had been hard to ignore that masculinity when she had to get close to him to help train Decoy. And even though she knew he'd been wounded, she hadn't de-tected anything while they worked together, except for possibly the occasional times he'd reached up to mas-sage his shoulder.

She was almost home, Chipper playfully tagging along beside her on her new pink leash, when her hack-les rose, and fear shimmied down her spine.

Pulling up short, she glanced around again, surprised that she was almost home. She'd been so involved in thinking about Shane that she hadn't realized how close she was to her house.

Her heart pounded in her chest as she peered at the woods surrounding the path and toward her backyard, searching for the source of her disquiet.

Nothing.

Sucking in a deep breath, there was no odor but pine

scent today unlike yesterday's very obvious cigarette smoke.

*You're imagining things*, she told herself, and as Chipper tugged at her leash and started barking and jumping, she squatted to rub the puppy's head. "Mommy is just being silly, Chipper," she said, and the puppy licked her face with doggy kisses, relieving a little bit of her upset.

She plodded on the last twenty yards or so, but once again skidded to a halt as she reached the alcove for her front door.

*You're not imagining that those flowerpots were moved*, she thought. There were obvious water rings where the pots had previously sat as well as some crushed and broken pansy stems along the edges. One plant even looked as if it had been messily replanted, and as she got closer, the loose dirt near it confirmed that something had happened to that pot.

Chipper tugged on her leash and sniffed around the pots, but Piper said, "Sit, Chipper."

The pup looked up, grinning and barking, and it took another "Sit" before she responded.

"Good girl," Piper said and offered her a treat from her jacket pocket.

After, she jammed her hands on her hips and surveyed the area again but saw nothing except a big red pickup as it turned the corner from the road for the DCA and slowly pulled in front of her house and parked. The driver's side door popped open. Shane stepped out and Decoy jumped down with him. They walked toward her, concern evident on Shane's features.

"You okay?" he asked as he approached. Decoy rushed to her and jumped up, demanding her attention

until Shane gave the sit command and the dog immediately responded as did Chipper, who cuddled next to
Decoy on the front step.

"Fine," she said but wrapped her arms around herself, and as his gaze tracked that move, she realized it
was a tell for him that things were anything but right.

He arched that brow again. "Are you sure? You look
a little...freaked."

Piper could lie again but knew it wouldn't fly with
him. She motioned to the flowerpots on the cement
by the path to her front door. "Someone messed with
these pots, and yesterday I smelled cigarette smoke as
I walked home. I feel like I'm being watched."

Shane nodded and did a slow pivot, peering all
around before walking to the edge of her driveway,
Decoy tagging along behind him as she kept a short
leash on Chipper to keep her close.

Shane squatted by the edge and Decoy bent his head
to smell the ground beside the driveway, then began to
jump up and down, as if he sensed something.

"Good boy. Sit," he said and when the dog responded,
he rubbed the dog's head in reward.

He straightened, looked over his shoulder at Piper,
and pointed to the grass where she could see some
tracks. "I'm guessing you came this way from the
DCA?"

She nodded. "I did. I like the walk when the weather
is nice."

Shane peered all around and the ghost of a smile
spread across his lips. "Beautiful scenery," he said and
then glanced her way again.

"It is. I'm probably just imagining it," she said, but that answer didn't seem to satisfy him.

He walked along the edge of the driveway, perusing the ground, Decoy beside him, as if they were searching for more footprints. With a shake of his head, he walked back to her, Decoy bounding behind him happily. Chipper strained at her leash until the little pup settled in next to her new best friend.

"Nothing there, but someone could have walked up from the road. Do you keep a key under the pot?"

She shook her head. "No. Emma has a key. No one else needs to get in," she said and bit her lower lip, well aware of what those words told him.

He nodded. "Okay. Maybe it was just someone hoping to find a key and make an easy score."

"Or maybe I'm just freaking out over nothing. That kind of stuff doesn't really happen in Jasper," she said.

"That kind of stuff can happen anywhere. Doesn't Emma have troubled teens at the DCA?" he argued.

"They would never do something like that. They're good boys who just need a little guidance," she said and poked him in the chest to emphasize her point.

He snared her finger. "Got it, Piper. But maybe you should think about putting in a security system or one of those video cameras."

Even though she wanted to again say that things like that weren't necessary in Jasper, she was still too worried about the possibility that he was right. And rather than argue with him, she said, "I'll think about it."

His nod was slow, hesitant. "Okay. Do you need me to check inside before you go in?"

She stared back toward her door, but it seemed secure. "I'll be okay."

He nodded but didn't move so she ignored him and went to her door. She tried the handle. Still locked. She opened the door and took a tentative step inside, peered around. Everything seemed as it should be, but just in case, she didn't close her front door as she did a slow reconnoiter of her ranch home, going from room to room, Chipper at her side, before returning to the front door.

Shane still stood there at the end of the alcove, solid as any rock from the nearby Idaho mountains. Decoy was at his side, patiently waiting.

She forced a smile she wasn't feeling and waved to let him know she was okay and as a goodbye.

He returned the wave and walked back to his pickup with Decoy. The dog jumped in first, he got in, and they drove away.

Piper closed the door, double-locked it and leaned against the security of her metal door.

She peered around her home, circled around the rooms again, making sure to check that all the windows were locked, and that the sliding doors to her back deck were secured. She paused to take in the view from those doors: the nearby woods; the meadow she traversed so often on her way to get to the DCA; and the mountains with their frosting of late spring snow. A beautiful view, but today it brought a sense of isolation and loneliness.

Until Chipper jumped up on her leg, demanding attention.

"Yes, girl. I see you," she said and picked up the puppy.

The warmth of that little body and affectionate licks along her face shook off more of those feelings. She finished her walk around the house, went to her bedroom and changed out of her work clothes. To wash away any lingering negative emotions, she took a long hot shower and after changed into comfortable clothes and went into the kitchen to make herself and Chipper a quick dinner, the puppy at her side.

Stomach full, she settled in to watch a rom-com with the puppy tucked against her in bed. As the movie ended, she was feeling infinitely safer and a lot less lonely thanks to Chipper's company. Finally relaxed, she took Chipper out to the back deck so she could relieve herself. Nothing happening there. Absolutely nothing.

Breathing an easier sigh, she tugged on Chipper's leash and the pup immediately responded and followed Piper back into the house and her bedroom.

As Chipper obediently snuggled into her new doggy bed with a toy and Piper slipped into her own bed, she had only one more wish for that night: that it would be as easy for her to learn to deal with Shane and the maelstrom of emotions he roused in her.

The sound of a car engine intruded in the quiet of the night, but it didn't move on the way it would with a passing vehicle. And then the engine noise suddenly stopped.

Worry crept into her again. She snagged her cell phone in case she had to call for help, slipped out of bed and tiptoed to her front window.

A now familiar red pickup truck sat there, Decoy in the passenger seat.

That maelstrom of emotions spun ever faster, especially as Shane bent and looked out the window toward the house. As their gazes locked, she had no doubt that he'd do whatever he needed in order to make sure she was safe, including sitting there all night if it was necessary.

She'd always been an independent woman, but she had to admit that the sight of him brought...relief.

But she told herself not to get too used to it because Shane would soon be gone.

# Chapter Four

She was nothing but a silhouette in the front window until she snapped on a light, illuminating her face and body. She wore an oversize brown T-shirt emblazoned with the DCA's German shepherd logo.

No worry on her face, only confusion and possibly relief as she raised her cell phone, and his phone rang.

He answered and she said, "What are you doing here?"

"I couldn't sleep and decided to take a drive. Figured I'd drop by to make sure everything was okay with you." Even though everything wasn't okay with him thanks to the nightmare that had woken him from the first semi-sound sleep he'd had in days.

"I'm…okay. You really didn't have to come by," Piper said.

She was right. He didn't really have to come by, but the short drive had helped to clear his brain of the lingering memories from his nightmare.

"I just wanted to make sure you were fine," he said, which was the truth. He really was worried about what might be happening with Piper. He'd seen no evidence that anything was going on, but Piper had been well and truly freaked out that something was wrong.

"I am. Thank you. Have a good night," she said and did a little wave.

He returned the wave and started up the car but waited until she had snapped off the light and disappeared from view before he drove off and back to the campground where his RV was parked.

"We're home, Decoy," he said and popped out of the pickup, Decoy quickly following him into the RV. He paused by the kitchen area to make sure Decoy still had fresh water and then pushed through to the back of the RV and his bedroom.

The sheets and comforter were a tangle he straightened out before stripping and climbing back into bed. A chill spring breeze, tinged with the scent of pine and fir, swept through the open windows of the RV. The breeze was strong enough to rustle the branches of the evergreens and a nearby stand of aspens.

He breathed in deeply, the scent calming. The soft whisper of the breeze and sounds of the branches soon lulled him to sleep again.

But other sounds and smells soon intruded again. The roar and heat that had filled the air when the car bomb had gone off. The rain of concrete and glass that became a deluge as the building collapsed on him and the soldiers he had been training.

The deafening silence that had followed as he lay there, his body aching in so many places he couldn't tell where one hurt began and another ended. The slow awakening of sound: the ringing in his ears; the calls of searchers; the screams and cries of the wounded. Pain sluggishly came to life as well and became focused on his right shoulder, which howled in agony.

He had been screaming. Calling out in the hopes of being found until he was hoarse and drained of energy. He'd passed out but woken to the bark of a dog. Decoy's bark. A lick on his hand and soft fur beneath his palm.

He woke up then, the sheets tangled all around him again. Decoy standing at the side of the bed, nudging his hand. Finding him once more. Saving him again as Shane moved over in the bed and patted the space beside him.

Decoy jumped up as commanded and snuggled into Shane's side, his presence and warmth comforting. Bringing him peace as he finally drifted off and slept.

THE GROUND BENEATH the tent was hard. Unyielding as he tried to get comfortable.

The only thing that made the small space of the tent habitable was the breeze blowing in through the open tent flaps.

*Just a little bit more time*, he told himself, only he suspected it would be longer than he would like.

He had thought he could get into the woman's home and search it right away, but so far he'd had no luck. Which meant he had to find somewhere more comfortable than the tent to stay in.

He'd been watching the place and had seen her coming and going. Pretty thing. David had been a lucky man.

*Well, lucky except for dying on that mission,* he thought.

He didn't want any problems with the woman, just

what he was entitled to and David had taken from him and Buck. That's all he wanted, but so far he was striking out.

And now there was a man around. He'd seen him stop and help the woman after he'd tried to find a key to get into the house. The man had been there tonight as well, damn it. He'd seen him when he'd been hiding in the woods nearby, hoping to figure out how and when he'd be able to get into the home.

Not anytime soon with the woman obviously worried something was happening and the man dropping by way too often.

He'd have to wait it out. Give it a couple of days or more for them to relax so he could find an opening for getting into the house.

David owed him and he intended to get what was his. Once he did, he'd have enough money to finally get on with his life.

He just needed to get what David had given his wife. He was sure she had it and he intended to get it back no matter what it took.

THE LICK OF a tongue along the underside of her jaw woke Piper from a deep sleep.

"G'morning, Chipper," she said and rubbed the puppy's head.

The puppy jumped up on her midsection and continued licking Piper's face. "I love you, too," she said, but nature was calling. Probably as well for the puppy.

She hopped from bed and quickly relieved herself, then clipped a leash on Chipper's collar and walked her into the backyard, where the puppy decided to nose around the potted plants, exploring.

Piper shivered in the chill of the morning air and wrapped her arms around herself to ward off the cold. "Chipper," she said sharply, drawing the puppy's attention, not that the puppy would understand.

"Sit," she said, and the pup obeyed. Smiling, she rubbed Chipper's head, earning that corgi smile in her tan-and-white face. It dragged a smile to her lips and a laugh.

She was surprised she could laugh after what had happened yesterday, but her spirit was lighter today. Not as worried, she thought as she glanced around her yard and saw that everything seemed normal.

It was a beautiful mid-April morning. The sun had just risen, painting the meadow behind her home with shades of rosy-pink and yellow light that brightened the colors of the wildflowers.

A tug on the leash drew her attention to Chipper, who had walked off the deck and was finally relieving herself on the nearby grass. She scratched and kicked up the ground in the area, marking her territory in typical canine scrape behavior.

"Come, Chipper," she said and swayed her palm in her direction, trying to reinforce the verbal command with the hand signal.

The puppy sat, ears perked up, and Piper repeated the command.

The dog immediately came to her side and Piper scooped her up, rewarding her with her attention. Once they were back inside, the sliding door locked behind them, she grabbed a treat from a canister on her kitchen counter and gave it to Chipper.

Removing her leash and letting Chipper settle into a dog bed in the living room, Piper rushed into the shower to get ready for another day at the DCA.

*Another day with Shane*, she thought as she washed.

It was hard to deny that maybe part of the reason she wasn't as worried was that she knew Shane was around.

But Shane wasn't going to be around forever. His training program was scheduled to last four weeks and then he'd be off for more intensive training with a search and rescue group. Not that the DCA couldn't provide that training since they often did. Emma had been working with a local group, Mountaintop SAR, and Dillon Diaz, one of the members of the Jasper PD force, to improve their SAR techniques and keep abreast of any new methods.

But Shane would be leaving, she reminded herself as she dressed, leashed Chipper and made the short walk from her home through the meadow to the DCA.

Unlike the other day, she had no sense of being watched. Detected no odors that were out of the ordinary. If anything, it was just another beautiful day, filled with the fresh scents of pine and fir, the rich colors of the evergreens and aspens in the nearby stands of trees and up on the mountain, and the wildflowers.

The ground was still moist with morning dew and wet the hem of her jeans as she walked. Luckily, she'd worn her waterproof boots to keep her feet dry and warm.

As she arrived at the DCA, she caught sight of Tashya coming out of Emma's home. Tashya was one of the young people whom Emma had fostered as a way to honor the Danielses, who had fostered her. Since Tashya's return from vet tech school in Boise, the young woman had been living with Emma. A second later, Tashya's boyfriend, Jason Wright, also came out of the house.

"Good morning, Tashya. Jason," she said, smiling at the handsome young man who had also been one of Emma's fosters and was now a rookie police officer with the Jasper PD.

"Good morning, Piper," they both answered in unison, but Jason quickly added, "I just stopped by to have breakfast, but it's time I headed to work."

He dropped a quick kiss on Tashya's lips and rushed to his car, leaving Piper and Tashya to start their morning routine. They checked in on their rescued puppies and the dogs in the kennels. Tashya remained behind with them while Piper went to check in with Emma and Barbara to see if there was anything new for the day.

As she walked out of the DCA offices with Emma, Shane pulled up in his red pickup. He parked and hopped out, Decoy following behind him.

He sauntered to them, his walk that of a man confident in his own skin. His blue gaze warmed as it settled on her. In a morning-husky voice, he said, "Good morning, Piper. Emma."

"Morning," she said and clasped her hands before her, unsettled by his attention.

"Morning, Shane. How are you today?" Emma said, looking between the two of them as if to decipher what was happening.

"I'm fine. Looking forward to today's training session since I learned so much yesterday," he said and once again glanced at her.

"Good," Emma quickly said. "I hope you won't mind that Officer Callan will be joining you today."

"Not at all. Anything for local law enforcement," he said and rubbed Decoy's head as the dog sidled up to his leg and sat.

"Then let's get going," Piper said and gestured in the direction of the training ring.

SHANE FOLLOWED PIPER into the ring, and they were soon repeating and reinforcing the commands they had worked on the day before. The "Sit" and "Look at me" commands, both verbal and hand signals.

To his pleasure, Decoy immediately responded to the commands, earning his rewards and Shane's affection as he complied.

"Good boy, Decoy. Good boy," he said, getting down on one knee to rub the dog's head and a special spot that he'd discovered behind his floppy ears.

The sound of a vehicle approaching drew their attention.

A Jasper PD police car pulled up and two officers stepped out of the vehicle along with a black-and-white shepherd dog.

Piper walked to the fence to greet them, and he trailed behind her.

"Shane. Meet Officers Callan and Diaz," Piper said.

Shane shook their hands. "Shane Adler. Nice to meet you."

"Ava," the pretty officer said. Her hair was pulled back into a tight bun as taut as her smile, clearly uneasy.

"Dillon," the other officer said. They were of a like height and build and his hazel-green eyes were filled with laughter as he gestured to the dog at his side. "This is Bentley, my unofficial K-9."

"Dillon's part of the local SAR group, Mountaintop," Piper explained.

"I understand you're interested in SAR," Dillon said.

"I am," Shane confirmed. "Decoy's very good at finding things and I'm hoping we can use those skills to help."

"Just like we're hoping that Ava can learn to work with Lacey," Piper said, clearly hoping to draw the young woman into the conversation since she'd been standing there awkwardly during the exchange.

"I hope so," Ava said, but it was obvious she was less than happy with the situation.

"It'll be fine, Ava," Dillon said, not that it relieved any of her anxiety.

"If it works out Chief Walters will be happy and if it doesn't, Captain Rutledge will be pleased, so I guess you're right," she said with a shrug of slim shoulders.

Dillon laughed and shook his head. "You nailed that right, Ava. If you'll excuse me, I have to run. Brady will be back later to pick you up," he said and walked back to the police car.

"Emma is going to bring Lacey over for you, Ava. She's a wonderful German shepherd we've trained here at the DCA," Piper explained. "You can work with her so she learns to listen to you while Shane works with Decoy and I train this little girl here," she said and bent to scoop up Chipper.

The ghost of a smile drifted across Ava's face at

the sight of the little puppy. She reached out and patted her head. "She's a cutie. Is she one of the puppies Macon rescued?"

"She is. We've been training them and thanks to the newspaper article, we've placed them with various families in town," Piper explained.

"Good to hear," she said just as Emma came over with a German shepherd.

"Officer Callan. Nice to see you," Emma said and shook Ava's hand.

"Ava, please," the young woman said.

"Meet Lacey. She's a two-year-old German shepherd. Friendly. Attentive. She's good at finding things, so we hope that'll be a help to you and Jasper PD," Emma explained and rubbed Lacey's long brown-and-tan fur.

"I hope so," Ava said, but it was clear to him, and probably also to Emma and Piper, that the young officer was less than pleased at being paired with Lacey.

"Great," Emma said and handed over Lacey's leash to Ava. "I'll leave you to it," she said with a broad, welcoming smile, obviously hoping to put the woman at ease.

"Let's get to work and welcome, Ava," Piper said. "We're really looking forward to having you with us."

The young woman forced a smile but nodded and slipped under the fence railing to join them, Lacey at her side.

In no time they were going through the first commands they'd taught Decoy, reinforcing those commands for his dog. Letting Ava bond with Lacey, who already understood the instructions and teaching them to Chipper, who was a little ball of energy and those Corgi smiles that could melt any heart.

Like they were melting Ava's together with the clear affection that Lacey immediately had for the young officer. By the time the other police officer showed up to take Ava back to police headquarters, a bond had clearly been developing between the officer and Lacey, and even with Piper. The officer seemed more relaxed around her.

Unlike how he was around Piper.

He seemed attuned to every little nuance about her. The way she'd rake her fingers through her hair to pull it off her face as she worked. The flush that would sometimes paint her cheeks when their gazes collided. The gentle but firm way she had with the animals as she reinforced the commands.

When the officers left, it was just the two of them in the ring, but instead of continuing there, Piper motioned to the agility course behind the training area.

"Ready to try something different?"

He was sure her idea of different would present a challenge, but he liked that. He liked how she made him feel and as he walked with her to the course, he realized he'd follow her anywhere. He hadn't planned on that, but some said God laughed at men who made plans.

Still, this unplanned attraction was downright scary. Possibly even more scary than the dreams that came way too often.

But the military had taught him not only how to plan but how to handle it when things went south, so he'd find a way to handle Piper and keep them both from getting hurt.

## Chapter Five

They spent the last hours of the day working on the agility course, letting Decoy explore the various obstacles on the course. An A-frame ramp, seesaw and elevated dog walk.

Piper was pleased with how easily Decoy handled those challenges and took Shane and Piper over to what were sometimes more difficult elements. A tunnel, chute and tire jump.

Decoy hesitated at the entry to the tunnel, but then pushed through and actually seemed to enjoy it with her at one end encouraging and Shane at the other end with a treat and affection. The chute, with its long tail of nylon where the dog was basically running blind, frightened Decoy, putting an end to the training session.

"Easy, boy," Shane said and kneeled on one knee to calm Decoy. "Easy."

Decoy settled down, especially as Chipper edged close to the older dog, demanding attention, which Decoy gave, licking the pup and placing a paw on her head to keep her down.

Piper laughed, enjoying the interaction between the two dogs. "They're so good together."

"They are. And Chipper's a fast learner," Shane said and straightened.

She was hit again by all that imposing masculinity, but also by the tenderness he showed toward the dogs and his restraint around Ava. The young officer had clearly been standoffish, hiding behind a wall she'd built around herself.

Shane hadn't pushed, as if knowing that would only make her build that wall higher. Maybe because he had his wall as well. She'd seen it at times when they were getting too close, both physically and emotionally.

Like they were now.

"Decoy's a fast learner as well. I'm sure that by the time we're done with training, Decoy will be able to handle all these obstacles," Piper said, building her own wall so she could handle the fact that Shane and Decoy would one day be leaving.

"I think it's time to call it a day," she said. The agility course had tested Decoy and being with Shane was testing her.

"I think so, too," he said and when he met her gaze, it was obvious he was feeling much the same.

"See you tomorrow," she said and rushed from the agility course, but she could feel his eyes on her as she entered the DCA offices.

He was gone by the time she finished chatting with Barbara and Emma and started the walk home.

Her mind was filled with satisfaction as she thought of the progress they'd made with all the dogs. With how Ava had finally let her in, just a little. Of Shane and how quickly he was learning.

Shane. Shane. Shane.

Stupid to think about it since, as she'd told him, he'd be leaving once his training was done.

She drove him from her thoughts, telling herself to be on the lookout for anything out of the ordinary as she approached her home. But there was nothing. No tracks except those of her own coming and going through the meadow and the scents of pine and fir as a spring breeze swept across a nearby stand of trees.

Nothing happening near her home, she thought as she walked around to her door.

Well, nothing except Shane sitting in his red pickup truck in front of the house.

He waved at her. Decoy barked a greeting, which had Chipper straining on her leash to go visit her friend.

Piper relented. She walked to the pickup and leaned on the edge of the open door. "You don't have to do this, Shane."

"You're right. I don't. I just wanted to make sure you're okay," he said and peered around at their surroundings.

"Nothing as far as I can see. Maybe I was just imagining it," Piper said, glancing back at her house and then tracking his gaze to look all around.

"Maybe," he said and clenched his fingers on the steering wheel. Facing her, he said, "I'll wait until you get in. Let me know you're okay."

He wouldn't relent, so she nodded and walked to her front door. Unlocked it and left it open as she had the other day. Once inside, she checked all around, but much like in the meadow, there was nothing to cause alarm.

She went back to the front door and waved at Shane. Called out, "All good here."

"Good. See you tomorrow," he replied, then gave a brief chop of his hand as a wave and drove away.

"Tomorrow," she whispered to no one.

Time to grab a bite, take a shower and relax so she could be ready for tomorrow and another day with Shane.

As THEY HAD in the past, the nightmares subsided with Decoy at his side. The warmth and weight of his body brought a sense of safety, much like they had as Decoy stayed with him while his Army colleagues dug him out of the rubble of the building they'd been using for training. He had only been able to touch Decoy's nose, feel his soft breath and the lick of his tongue, but that had been enough to keep him from feeling lost and alone.

With the nightmares under control, he'd had more energy and focus during the training sessions at the DCA, and it showed as they neared the end of the first week.

"You two are learning quickly," Piper said as Shane ran through the various verbal and hand commands and Decoy obeyed. Earlier in the day they had taken a few runs through the agility course, even the dreaded chute that had so terrified Decoy on the second day of training.

"We have a good instructor," he said, then bit his lower lip, worried it sounded too much like flirting.

Bright splotches of color erupted on Piper's creamy cheeks, and she downplayed his compliment. "It's easy when I have a dog like Decoy to work with," she said, and then quickly tacked on, "and you."

The color deepened on her cheeks, and she looked away, obviously embarrassed.

Luckily, they were both saved from what could have led to even more awkwardness by Ava's arrival with Emma and Lacey.

"How's it going?" Emma asked, immediately picking up on the vibes between the two of them.

"Good," they both said simultaneously, earning an arched brow from both Emma and Ava.

"Good," Emma said and jerked her head in the direction of the agility course where they'd been working earlier that morning. "Are you done over there?"

"We are. I was just thinking of taking Shane and Decoy indoors so we can maybe work on some attack and protect commands since he's learning so quickly," Piper said.

Shane hadn't thought about teaching Decoy anything like that, but it certainly could come in handy if they were doing search and rescue in an area that wasn't secure.

"Wonderful. If you aren't going to be too late, I was thinking we could all grab a bite after the training. Shane? Ava? Are you up for it?" Emma said.

Shane glanced at Ava, who in the last week had become more comfortable around all of them. Because of that, he said, "I'd love to go."

Ava offered up a small smile before echoing his acceptance of the invite. "Sure. That would be nice."

"Great. I was thinking we could go to Bartwell Brewing. They've got some great local craft beers and the food's pretty good as well. Six o'clock," Emma said and dipped her head as if to end the discussion.

"Six o'clock," Ava said, then with Lacey on a leash beside her, followed Emma to the agility course.

"Determined, isn't she?" Shane said and ran a hand through his hair while watching the two women walk away.

Piper's gaze darkened, grew sad. "You could say that, or you could say that Emma just wants to help others."

Shane didn't think he needed help, but kept quiet, not wanting to push the issue. Tipping his head in the direction of the building where he'd seen the indoor ring earlier in the week, he said, "You mentioned something about attack and protect?"

Piper nodded. "Sure. Follow me."

PIPER AND EMMA had driven to Bartwell Brewing together as they did so often when they had a girls' night.

Shane's red pickup was parked near the mouth of the alley where the brewery was located in a huge warehouse just off Third Street and not far from the headquarters for the police department. Its proximity was one of the reasons that the brewery was such a popular place with local law enforcement. The craft beers and good food didn't hurt either.

As Emma and she walked in, Piper spotted a couple of police officers at a high-top table near the bar: Dillon Diaz and his best friend, Brady Nichols. Both Brady and Dillon had trained their dogs at the DCA and were regular visitors at the ranch. They smiled and waved as Emma and Piper walked past them to the back of the brewery where Shane sat at a table in the dining area.

He stood as they approached.

"Hi," Piper said, admiring how the dark blue Western shirt he wore accented his broad shoulders and lean midsection. The color magnified the intense blue of his eyes, which glittered brightly in the mellow light of the high-ceilinged warehouse building. Mother-of-pearl buttons barely held the fabric tight against the muscled width of his chest.

"Hi," he said, his voice slightly husky.

"Hi, Shane," Emma said cheerily from beside her and then peered around the brewery. "Have you seen Ava?"

"Not yet," Shane said at the same time that Piper's phone rang. Ava was calling.

"Hi there, Ava. We're in the back dining room."

"I'm sorry, but I won't be able to make it. Captain Rutledge wants Jason and me to work the night shift. Says we have to earn our stripes," Ava said, the exasperation apparent in her tone.

"Sorry to hear that. Sorry about Rutledge as well. I know he can be difficult," Piper said, staring at Emma and shaking her head in disgust.

"I have to learn to deal with him, right? But I am sorry. I was looking forward to tonight," the young officer said. When noise filtered in from behind her, she added, "Have to run."

Piper swiped to end the call and blew out a harsh breath. "Captain Rutledge is making Ava and Jason work tonight. Do you think it has to do with Ava training with us?"

"And Jason dating Tashya? Possibly," Emma said and took a seat at the table.

Piper and Shane joined her, Piper at her side and Shane across from them.

"I gather Rutledge is not a fan," Shane said just as a waitress came over with some menus.

"The craft beer list is on the back, and we also have an assortment of the usual in bottles or draft. Bud, Miller, Stella and the rest," the young woman advised and took a pad and pen out of her apron pocket.

"Anything you can recommend?" Shane asked Piper and Emma.

"I love the Mountaintop IPA, plus a portion of the sales go to our local search and rescue group. I'll take a pint of that," Piper said.

"The same," Shane and Emma said.

"I'll go get your drinks and be back for your food orders," the waitress replied and hurried off to place their orders.

Emma took only a quick look at the menu and laid it down on the table. "Burgers and steaks are always good here."

With a bob of his head, Shane said, "Sounds good."

The waitress returned a couple of minutes later with their drinks, and they placed their food orders and returned to their earlier conversation.

"What's up with Rutledge?" Shane asked, pressing the issue again.

Piper shared a look with Emma and said, "He's not a fan of the K-9 program at Jasper PD. If Chief Walters retires—"

"*When* he retires, Piper," Emma corrected. "I know Doug is looking forward to more free time."

"I GUESS THE captain is next in line to be chief?" Shane said, sensing the upset of both women over the Jasper PD officer.

Emma and Piper shared another look. One of disgust if he had to guess, which surprised him since both women were generally easygoing and friendly.

"He thinks he is, but truth be told, many of the officers have issues with him," Piper said with a wrinkle of her nose as if she was smelling something bad.

"We're hoping Chief Walters chooses someone else to take over," Emma added, and Shane understood what they weren't saying. Someone who would be supportive of the police department continuing the K-9 program and training with the DCA.

He raised his glass of beer in a toast. "To the DCA and a big thank-you for all you've taught me so far."

Both women smiled and joined in the toast. "To the DCA and to your success in an SAR group," Emma said.

Piper chimed in with "I second that," but Shane detected a momentary flicker of sadness in her gaze. As she met his, there was no doubting it from the emotion in those deep green eyes.

In their short week together, something had changed between them that had nothing to do with the K-9s or his plans to move on to possibly join a search and rescue group in Montana.

He decided a change of discussion was the best remedy for the sudden melancholy he was likewise feeling.

"How did you start the DCA?" Shane said, wondering what would have made two such bright and beautiful women dedicate themselves to such an out-of-the-ordinary life in the Idaho mountains.

Emma shrugged, but then launched into her story. "My foster dad was a K-9 officer with the Jasper PD. He helped train a lot of the dogs and officers in Jasper as well as in nearby police departments. My foster mom was very active in community affairs, including work with local animal shelters to try and get the animals rescued before they were put down. After they both died, I inherited money from an insurance payment, and it seemed right to use that money to honor them by continuing the work that they did with the dogs."

There was more to the story, he could tell, but suddenly Emma's phone rang and barely a second after Emma answered, the waitress came over with their meals.

The waitress was about to walk away, when Emma ended her call and said, "I'm going to have to take mine to go."

"I'll get you a container," the waitress said and hurried off.

"What's wrong?" Piper asked, brows knitted together with worry.

"Tashya says Gus the cat got into it with a fox. Gus won, but he got bit and Tashya needs help since Marie's busy with a horse that's foaling."

"I guess I'll get mine to go as well," Piper said.

"I can drive you," Shane said at the same time that Emma replied, "You stay."

Piper looked from one to the other and shrugged. "Okay. I can stay, that is if it's not a big deal to drive me home."

It was only about twenty minutes from his RV campground to Piper's home, but more importantly, he didn't want the night with Piper to end so soon.

"It's no big deal."

Except he could hear Gonzo's voice in his head chastising him. *Dude, it's totally a big deal because you have feelings for this woman.*

He didn't really know just what those feelings were, but he intended to take the time to find out, starting with tonight.

# Chapter Six

She was alone with Shane. Great.

Except she'd been alone with him various times during the week while they trained.

But this was different. This was a potentially monumental shift in the cornerstone of the wall she'd built around herself since David's death.

*You can get through this*, she told herself, as Shane asked, "How did you and Emma get to know each other?"

*Keep it to Emma and you*, she thought.

"We met in college and became fast friends. When I wasn't in school or interning for my degree, I'd visit with Emma and her mom."

Shane cut a piece of his steak slowly, clearly thinking about what to ask next. "Emma mentioned her dad died."

Since the information was public news based on various articles that had been written about her friend, she didn't feel she was betraying a confidence by sharing it. "Her foster dad, Rick, died in the line of duty. Rick and his wife, Susan, fostered Emma after she was removed from her home because of issues with domestic violence. She loved the Danielses, and sadly, her mom passed about a year after she finished college."

"I'm sorry to hear that," he said and forked up some of the French fries that had come with his meal.

An awkward silence followed. Emma suspected what he wanted to ask and yet he didn't, maybe because then she'd ask him about his background. Much like hers, it was forbidden territory, she suspected. Still, she wanted to know more about him.

"I've met Gonzo once or twice when he brought some of his teens to the DCA to work with us. How did the two of you become friends?"

"We met in basic training. We had both enlisted right out of high school after 9/11. We just hit it off and I knew I could always count on him to watch my six," Shane explained and swirled a French fry through a mound of ketchup on his plate.

Piper chewed on her burger thoughtfully, struggling with how to phrase what to ask. Somehow her mouth blurted it out before her brain could stop her. "Were you with him when…?"

Shane paused with the French fry halfway up to his mouth, then set it down. "I was. It was supposed to be a routine scouting mission to look for a small Taliban cell that had been terrorizing a nearby village. We were ambushed and luckily we didn't lose a man, but Gonzo was seriously injured. We didn't know how bad until later."

UNTIL THE DOCTORS had dealt with the immediate emergency and then loaded his buddy onto a plane headed for the Ramstein Air Base in Germany, so he could be treated at Landstuhl Regional Medical Center.

"He was lucky to survive," Piper said, and her gaze darkened once more, to a green like that of the deepest shadows in a forest.

She was thinking about her husband. The man who hadn't survived.

"I'm sorry about your husband," he said and immediately regretted it as tears shimmered in her gaze and one spilled down her cheek.

He reached into his jeans pocket for the handkerchief his father had always said he should carry because you never knew when you might need it. Handing it to her, he said, "It must have been hard for you."

She took the handkerchief and dabbed at her eyes. "It was. I was lucky to have Emma. She was a big help because I was so lost."

He knew the feeling well and something inside him made him share. "I was an expert sharpshooter and had been offered a position as a trainer. After Gonzo was hurt, it made me realize how fragile life was and so I took that position," he said and jabbed at the steak to finish it although it would probably taste like sawdust thanks to their conversation.

She reached out and laid a hand on his, stilling his almost angry motion.

"But you were hurt anyway and now here you are. With us," she said and soothed her thumb across his knuckles, the gesture surprisingly comforting.

"I am," he said, his tone more resigned than curt.

She did a slow nod and, with laser focus, settled her gaze on him. "When David died, I asked myself time and time again why it happened. It took a long time for me to realize that I was meant to go on a different journey than the one I had envisioned for myself."

"What had you envisioned?" he asked, needing to know more about this woman who intrigued him on so many levels.

"David and me. Babies. A small house in the suburbs. Teaching elementary school. I was an education major," she admitted freely, a Mona Lisa–like smile on her face. "And you?" she added.

"In truth?" he said and paused, digging deep into his soul for the answer. "I always wanted to be a soldier. Even before 9/11. As for family, I wanted what my parents had. Laughter. Love, only… There was never enough time for that after I enlisted."

She blew out a harsh laugh, as if chastising herself. "There never is 'enough time,'" she said, emphasizing the words by using her fingers to mimic quote marks. "Unless you make time for it."

"You don't think that's what I'm doing now?" he asked because in truth, he still wasn't sure what he was doing at the DCA. When Gonzo had mentioned it and he had spoken to Emma and then the leader of the Montana SAR group, it had seemed like something to try. Something to replace being a soldier only…

*Was it just another excuse to keep from really living?* he thought.

That Mona Lisa smile drifted across her lips once again, filled with compassion, sadness and possibly even resolve.

"I guess we'll find out," she said.

AN EXPECTANT QUIET filled the cab of the pickup as Shane and Piper did the short trip from the brewery to Piper's ranch house.

When Shane pulled into her gravel driveway, he killed the engine and sat there, gripping the wheel tightly before he faced her and said, "Let me walk you to the door."

"No need. I'll be fine," she said, but hesitated, torn because she didn't want the night to end.

"A gentleman always escorts a lady home," he said and before she could say anything else, he hopped out of the pickup and walked around to open her door.

When he held his hand out to her, she slipped hers into his. Comfort immediately filled her from the touch of his big, calloused hand. She slid down from the high cab of the truck to the ground. He continued to hold her hand as they walked to her house, releasing it only so she could fish her keys out of her purse and open her front door.

She faced him, looking up because of his much greater height. He was so big and strong and yet so gentle with Decoy, Chipper and her. Honorable. Intelligent. Caring. All of that called to her, scared her, so she reminded herself that Shane would leave one day.

"Thank you. No need for you to stick around," she said, and gestured to the peaceful quiet of the night.

Shane did a perusal of the area. "Looks like everything is fine. Nothing new happening, right?"

"Nothing new. I guess it was just kids or someone looking to make a quick buck like you said."

He nodded, jammed his hands in his jeans pockets

and rocked back and forth on his heels. "I guess it's good-night."

"I guess," she said, even though she was conflicted.

"Good night," he said and leaned down to brush a kiss across her cheek, but as he did so, she shifted her head, just the tiniest bit. But enough that his lips skimmed hers.

A jolt like that from a live wire surged through her, weakening her knees. She had to grab hold of his arm for support, and he steadied her by laying a gentle hand at her waist.

The kiss deepened, his mouth mobile on hers for only a second before he jerked away from her with a mumbled curse.

"I'm sorry. That shouldn't have happened," he said and stepped back, giving her breathing room that she totally needed.

She sucked in a deep breath and held it, bracing herself. Expelling the breath slowly, she said, "No need to apologize. We're both adults. We know what we're doing."

He arched a brow. "Do you? Because I sure don't. I don't know what I'm doing. Where I'm going. What I'm supposed to do with the rest of my life."

Which made him a very dangerous man. After years of living with David and his absences, his death, the last thing she needed was another man who might not be there one day.

"Good night, Shane. I'll see you in the morning for training. Just training," she said, then rushed into her home and closed the door. She leaned against it, counting the long seconds until she heard the car start and the crackle of the driveway gravel as he pulled out and away.

With a rough sigh, she shook her head to chastise herself for what had just happened, and double-locked the door. She walked all around her house, checking the windows and the sliding doors to make sure all was in order.

It was.

Chipper perked up as she caught sight of Piper, and she let the puppy out of the crate. The little dog came over to jump excitedly at her feet and bark. She picked her up and cradled her against her chest, earning doggy kisses all along her jaw.

"I love you, too, Chipper," she said with a laugh, the puppy's antics chasing away her earlier upset.

With a final rub of Chipper's head, she placed the pup down, leashed her and walked her out to the back deck so she could relieve herself. The puppy did her thing quickly and they came back in, locked up and went to her bedroom, where Chipper obediently headed straight to her doggy bed.

"Good girl, Chipper," she said and patted the dog's head.

A quick look around her room and check of the windows said she was safe.

Well, at least from her imaginary intruder.

Shane was a whole 'nother problem, but come morning, she'd set things back to right.

Shane was her client and nothing else.

THERE WAS NO missing the chill coming off Piper during the last week, Shane thought. She was all business, with none of the easy smiles and laughter that had gradually become part of their training sessions the week before.

They worked Decoy through all the verbal and hand signals and the dog instantly responded, earning his treats and attention to reinforce the behavior. They'd added some hide-and-seek games, placing bits of treats and clothing in various areas around the DCA compound. Finding the treats had been a slam dunk for Decoy, the clothing not so much, but Piper had said that in time and with training Decoy's skills would improve.

Chipper wasn't as quick with the commands, but then again, she was way younger than Decoy, but little by little the pup was learning.

Decoy had also been sailing through all the obstacles on the agility course, so much so that Emma had brought in some additional tunnels and taller, less steady ramps and seesaws to challenge his dog. At first Decoy had balked at the shaky footing on the seesaw, but by the end of the week he was going up and over it without issue.

Chipper not so much on the basic course with her short legs and sometimes shorter attention span. But Piper was patient with the puppy, who did finally manage to make it up and over the ramp and through the tunnel, but not the chute or seesaw.

That warmth in her attitude was also evident when Ava joined them to train. The young officer, who had been standoffish to start, had become friendlier and was quickly learning how to handle Lacey. It was also obvious the German shepherd had bonded with Ava and as the two of them walked away to return to the police station, Shane said, "Looks like things are going to work out with those two."

Piper tracked the officer and dog as their police cruiser drove away. "It does. Ava and Lacey will be a wonderful K-9 team. Chief Walters had a good idea to put them together."

Shane couldn't miss the note of affection that drifted into her tone at the mention of the chief. "You like him a lot, don't you?"

"I do. He saved Emma," she said and at his questioning glance, continued. "I'm not telling you anything you wouldn't know if you did an internet search on Emma and the DCA."

He did a slow nod. "I respect loyalty, Piper."

PIPER GUESSED HE was referring to more than just her relationship with Emma, but she ignored the inference to finish her story.

Scooping up Chipper, who had been growing restless, she said, "When Emma's foster dad died, she kind of lost it. She was only sixteen and she loved him. Respected him. She got involved with the wrong boy and ended up in trouble. Chief Walters helped put her back on the right path. Became like a second dad to her and to a lot of the kids that Emma has fostered over the years."

"Chief Walters sounds like a good man," Shane said and dipped his head.

"He is. He's been very supportive of Emma and the DCA. And his K-9 program at Jasper PD is one of the best in the area."

Shane smiled and rubbed Decoy's head as the dog

bumped his leg, as if wondering why they were just standing there instead of training.

"You and Emma are amazing instructors. You're doing great work with the dogs and the kids you help. Gonzo couldn't say enough nice things about you," he said.

She smiled at the mention of his friend, who was a strong supporter and a wonderful man from what she could tell. "Gonzo's the best."

"He is. I guess we're both lucky to have such good friends," he said, but when his bright blue gaze settled on hers, there was no doubt the last thing he wanted for them was to be friends.

"I think it's time to call it a day," she said, and before he could say anything else, she set Chipper back on the ground and hurried out of the training ring.

In no time Chipper and she had slipped between the kennels and barn and were walking through the meadow on the way home. Beneath her booted feet, the ground was a little soft from an overnight rain. A riot of color greeted her in the meadow since the rain had encouraged even more flowers to open.

The beauty of the nature around her filled her with peace as it always did. It had been one of the things that had kept her steady in the months after David's death. Well, that and Emma. She could never repay Emma enough for the support she had provided and this new life that gave her so much satisfaction.

She loved working with the dogs and meeting new people. Seeing people grow as they bonded with the canines. Seeing others open up, like Ava and, yes, Shane.

He'd been more closed off when he'd first arrived,

but during the first week he'd loosened up a little. Become more easygoing. Until the kiss, of course.

That had set them back to square one or maybe even further back, if that was possible.

As she rounded the corner of her house, she stopped short.

Her car door was ajar.

Hands on her hips, she did a slow pivot, inspecting the area all around her home.

No signs of anything else being out of the ordinary.

Chipper jumped onto her leg, demanding attention.

"Sit," she commanded sharply, and the puppy responded, her floppy ears, courtesy of the pit in her, perking up at Piper's tone.

"Good girl, Chipper," she said and bent to pat the dog's head.

Squatting there, she peered at the ground, searching the grass all around and focusing on a spot in the gravel near her car door.

Nothing.

She rose and walked over to the car. Just some fingerprints by the handle the way you might expect.

Just in case, she used the hem of her T-shirt to open the door.

The top edge of the inside door panel was slightly wet as if the door had been open during last night's light rain. She ran her finger along the weather stripping at the top of the door, which was also damp from being ajar.

Obviously, the door had been open since last night and no one had come by during the day. Which freaked her out to think about someone being out here, going through her car while she was asleep in the house.

Only there was nothing amiss inside the car. She kept her vehicle pristine and would have noticed anything.

Glancing around the area again, she ran through what she had done last night when she'd come home from dinner with Emma. She'd driven since Tashya had borrowed Emma's vehicle to take one of their dogs to the vet.

*I'm sure I closed it.* But her seat belt latch sometimes ended up between the door and her seat. Sure enough, the latch dangled close to the side of the seat since the seat belt hadn't retracted as it should have.

She slipped her key fob from the knapsack she usually carried to work and locked her car. Walking to her front door, where everything was as it should be, she shook her head to chastise herself for being silly.

There was only one threat she had to worry about: six-plus feet of a too-tempting Army vet.

## Chapter Seven

Shane was restless after that day's training session. Well, restless and intrigued about Emma as well as Piper. She had told him about her friend's history, but not much about herself.

He needed to know more about her.

Since Piper had mentioned the internet, he jumped online and did searches to find information on Emma and the DCA. As he read through the articles, he grew even more impressed with all that Emma had accomplished at the canine academy. But buried in the various articles and blogs that the DCA posted to offer tips on training and their staff were breadcrumbs about Piper.

How she was a military widow whose Marine husband had been killed in Iraq.

That she had moved from California to Idaho to join the DCA four years earlier.

It didn't take much to find out when her husband had died and that the DCA had likely been her refuge from memories of him.

He could understand her flight. *I'm doing the same thing, right?*

*Right, but when will you stop running?* the little voice in his head challenged.

He shut down his laptop and grabbed his keys. Right now, all he was running to was a nice cold pint of the wonderful IPA he'd had the other night at the brewery.

When he arrived, he noticed Officer Dillon Diaz alone at one of the high-top tables. He'd met the officer at the DCA when he'd come by to chat with Emma and Piper.

The officer waved as Shane walked in and he took it as an invitation to join him.

As he neared, he realized that the officer was having coffee and not a brew. "Officer Diaz. On duty?"

"Dillon, please, and yes. Just keeping an eye on things," the other man said.

Shane did a quick look around, but everything seemed fine.

"Problems?" he asked.

With a quick dip of his head, Dillon said, "Some. A few cars broken into. Cash taken from a tip jar here in the brewery at the end of the night. Small stuff."

Which made Shane think of the little things that had been bothering Piper and his suspicions about the pots at her front door. For a moment he wanted to share that info with the officer, but since Piper hadn't mentioned anything new in the last week, he thought better of it.

"Anything I should keep an eye out for?" he said and gestured to a waitress to come over.

"It's probably just some kids out for a thrill, but if you notice any strangers, present company excluded, of course, or anything out of the ordinary, you should give us a call," he said and sipped his coffee.

Shane smiled and laid a hand on his chest. "Glad you're not including me."

Dillon chuckled and it reached up into his hazel-green eyes. "I've seen you and your dog. Dogs are a great judge of character. So are Emma and Piper. If they're cool with you, so am I."

"Glad to hear. I understand you're part of the local search and rescue group," Shane said, and after the waitress had placed the beer on the high-top, he paid her, including a generous tip.

"I am. Bentley and I trained at the DCA and while we're not officially part of the Jasper PD K-9 squad, we help out when needed." He gestured to Shane with his coffee cup. "I hear your dog is really catching on quickly. We're always looking for new members to help out. You can't imagine how many lost hikers and stranded skiers we have."

"I appreciate the confidence," he said, but he'd already been in contact with another SAR group in Montana. Despite that, the seed had been planted and took root. After all, he wanted to be able to spend time with Gonzo when he could, and Jasper wasn't all that far away. The trip from Boise to Montana was over twice as long, nearly eight hours. Too far from Gonzo.

*Too far from Piper, too?* the little voice challenged.

The words left his mouth before he could rein them in. "I'll think about it. Thanks."

Dillon smiled and finished the last of his coffee. He slipped his police baseball cap on his head, tipped the edge of it with his finger and said, "I hope you'll stay."

Shane laughed and shook his head at the man's determination. "Like I said, I will think about it."

With a little salute, Dillon walked away, leaving Shane to finish his beer and consider the request.

If anyone had asked him two weeks ago if he'd even consider settling down in a small town like Jasper, he might have said no.

But after the chaos of multiple deployments in Iraq and Afghanistan, the peace and quiet of Jasper was a blessing. It was nice to fall asleep to the sound of branches gently waving in the breeze and the burble of water along the edges of the nearby Salmon River. To wake to the morning air, still chill in mid-April.

He loved the quiet, except in those moments when the nightmares came. It was in those moments that he could have used the noises of the city to drown out the memories of war. Of friends injured and lost. Of the building exploding into bits around him, pouring down on him to trap him in a grave of twisted wire, broken cinder block and smoldering wood.

*Enough*, he warned himself, tossing off the memories the way Decoy shook water from his fur after a morning dip in the river.

Grabbing his beer, he chugged the last of the IPA and set the glass down with a loud thump.

It was time to head back to his RV. Decoy needed to be let out one last time for the night.

But as he walked down the alley, his hackles rose, almost as if someone had a bead on him.

He stopped and looked back in the direction of the brewery. A few patrons lingered along the far side of the building, smoking. None seemed to be paying any attention to him.

He started back toward his car, but the disquiet lingered, spurred by what Dillon had told him earlier and the incidents at Piper's the week before.

Little incidents. Little thefts. But stack up all those little things and they could sometimes become bigger things. Dangerous things.

Because of that, he intended to make one quick stop before he went home.

HE DIDN'T KNOW who this guy was or why he kept on showing up. But regardless of the why, he could be trouble.

He recognized a fellow military man when he saw one. The guy would be able to defend himself and Lambert's wife. Not that he intended to go after her. At least not when this dude and his dog were around.

Dogs were trouble, too. For some reason, they didn't seem to like him, and truth be told, he didn't like them very much either.

Since he'd overheard the police officer calling in to say he'd be doing some extra patrols around town and its outskirts, he'd have to lay low tonight.

Besides, Lambert and her little dog would be back at work in the morning, giving him plenty of time to get into her house and try to find the relics that Lambert had sent to her from Iraq.

Both he and his buddy Buck had been with Lambert on a mission when they'd found them and secured the ancient carvings and a gold bracelet. But the treasures had disappeared after Lambert had been killed and they'd gone back to get them.

He had no doubt Lambert had taken them for himself and sent them to his wife.

Now he intended to get them back no matter what it took.

But not tonight. He'd bide his time and try again tomorrow and the day after that if necessary.

It had cost him too much not to keep on trying to find them.

PIPER WOKE TO a dreary and chilly morning. It had been raining on and off all night, and a lingering drizzle and clouds made it the kind of day where she just wanted to pull the covers up over her head and stay in bed.

But she couldn't because she had obligations to Shane and Decoy. She never shirked obligations no matter how difficult it was for her to be around Shane.

Normally she'd have more of a buffer since she would only train each client for a few hours each day over the course of a month or more depending on what the client needed. But a client had cancelled at the last minute and Shane only had four weeks to spend at the DCA which was why they were training so intensely.

Because of that, both Shane and Decoy had made incredible progress over the course of the last two weeks. Decoy was a natural at finding things, probably thanks to his Lab/hound blood. But not all good searchers made capable rescue dogs, especially in dangerous conditions like those in a building collapse or finding people in the aftermath of mudslides, earthquakes or avalanches.

In those situations, a dog had to be unafraid of things like uneven ground, crevices or the kind of rubble in which Shane had been buried in Afghanistan.

*Shane*, she thought with a sigh.

Much like Decoy, he had shown himself to be a perfect candidate for a search and rescue group. He was calm and patient with Decoy, and the dog obeyed him without question. The bond between them was unquestionable and she had no doubt that Decoy would go into a dangerous situation if Shane requested it. But she also knew Shane would not endanger Decoy unnecessarily, and with his military experience, he'd be adept at sizing up risks and how to proceed.

As she lay in bed, her mind raced with ideas for this week's training session. They'd added more obstacles to the agility course, but with the rain it would be uncomfortable to be outdoors today so any work outside or on the trails around the DCA would have to wait. Not to mention it would be muddy in the outdoor rings.

The indoor ring would have to do for today and she had an idea of just what to do besides some attack and protect training.

Peering at her watch, she realized she should get moving if she was going to set up that training for Shane and Decoy.

She hurried her morning routine, including a quick walk along the road with Chipper, who was almost completely housebroken.

In no time they were at the DCA and by then the rain had gotten heavier from the earlier morning mist. They rushed into the DCA offices, where Barbara had yet to arrive, but the lights were on in Emma's office. She walked over to find her friend working at her desk.

"Good morning. You're in early," Piper said and leaned on the doorjamb. Chipper settled down at her feet.

"I had some paperwork to do and figured a rainy

day like today would be the perfect time to take care of that. You're here early also," Emma pointed out and leaned back in her chair.

"I thought we'd do something different because of the weather," Piper said and tilted her head in the direction of the indoor ring.

"Need help?" Emma asked, clearly eager for a break from the paperwork.

"Sure. I was going to do some more hide-and-seek exercises as well as attack and protect," Piper said.

Emma nodded and got up from her chair. "You could also think about starting to train Decoy on how to alert Shane when he finds something."

She hadn't thought about that and dipped her head to confirm. It was important Decoy learn to communicate that he'd found something important. "Sounds good. We can work on that alerting today and then test Decoy on it when we do hide-and-seek on the trails."

As they left Emma's office, Barbara hurried in, juggling a dripping umbrella, her oversize purse and a box from the local bakery.

They rushed over to help her with the items and Barbara smiled. "Thank you! I almost lost the doughnuts on the way in."

"Doughnuts? Nom, nom," Emma said and placed the box on the small table in the narrow entryway where they kept coffee and tea for clients.

Barbara smoothed the fabric of her loose shirt down and sighed. "I know I should be watching what I eat, but it's so dreary and I thought we'd need a pick-me-up."

Piper laid a reassuring hand on Barbara's shoulder. "Barbara, you are perfect the way you are."

Emma's assistant smiled. "That's what my Bob always says," she said, referring to her husband. She lived in town with him and her daughter, Samantha, who was away at college.

"And he's right," Emma chimed in, then snagged a doughnut from the box and held it up. "Thank you so much for these. They will hit the spot on this rainy day."

"You are so welcome. Time to get to work," Barbara said, then shrugged out of her rain jacket and went into her office.

"I'll text Shane and let him know we're inside today," Piper said and after she did so, they walked into the indoor ring and to an equipment locker that contained various items that they used for their lessons.

As they hauled out the long-armed glove and padded suit for the attack and protect lessons, Chipper chased after them, playfully attempting to catch the straps from the suit. "Silly dog," Piper said and affectionately rubbed Chipper's head. "Now, sit," she said, and when the puppy obeyed, she offered up a treat.

Emma bent to pat the dog's head and Chipper ate up the attention, hopping up on Emma's legs.

Emma rubbed Chipper's ears and the dog barked and continued to hop up and down on her legs.

"You're such a cutie," Emma said and laughed.

Piper couldn't argue with her friend. Chipper was adorable and turning out to be a wonderful companion. "She is a great buddy. Smart. She's caught on to all the commands so far."

"Corgis are very intelligent, and pits are friendly and gentle contrary to all the bad press," Emma said and straightened.

Chipper immediately sat at her feet, smiling, as if approving of Emma's comments.

It dragged laughs from both the women but then Chipper barked and took off toward the door of the indoor training area, jerking the leash from Piper's hands.

Shane and Decoy stood there, and Chipper was immediately climbing all over the older dog, who patiently accepted the attention.

Shane bent, took hold of Chipper's leash and walked over to them.

Raindrops glistened on the longer strands of his close-cropped hair and the shoulders of his rain jacket. "Nasty day out there," he said.

"It is, but we'll be comfortable in there," Piper said and gestured to the ring.

SHANE SURE HOPED SO. They'd been in the indoor ring another day for attack and protect lessons, but there had been something claustrophobic about it. Maybe because it reminded him of the area where he'd been training his men immediately before the IED blast that had nearly taken his life. Not to mention that in the enclosed space, it made it that much harder to ignore Piper's physical presence and how it made him feel.

Despite his misgivings, he said, "We will."

Emma gestured to the padded suit on the floor of the ring. "I guess I'll go and let you guys get started."

After Emma walked out of the room, Piper explained to Shane what they would be doing that day, finishing up with the training on alerting Shane.

Shane narrowed his gaze and glanced at Decoy, who was lying down calmly beside him, Chipper resting next to him. "You want Decoy to alert me?" he said, wanting to confirm what he'd just heard.

Piper nodded. "Yes. There may be situations where Decoy will sense a danger you might not or when he finds something. Dogs can detect gas leaks or even someone who is going to have a seizure because of their acute sense of smell."

"Seizures have a scent?" Shane asked, truly puzzled.

Piper shrugged. "There are some studies that seem to show there's some kind of smell, possibly the smell of fear."

Shane cocked his head to the side and peered at the two dogs. "Amazing. So how are we going to do this?"

"First, we do the attack and protect. Afterward we'll start by having Decoy find hot dogs and toys we hide around the ring. Once he's found an object, we can teach him to sit and bark to let us know."

"Okay. I'm ready if you are," he said, although he didn't much care for the attack and protect classes. They had involved irritating Decoy with a glove until he reacted with anger and attacked it. The irritation had been combined with an attack command.

Decoy had always been a patient animal and it had taken quite a lot to push the dog to attack. It made him wonder if Decoy would ever be able to attack if needed, not that he ever wanted to be in that kind of situation again. He'd been in enough mayhem and destruction in the military.

"Just let me take Chipper out to Barbara," she said, then snagged the leash for her puppy and walked him out. When she returned, she walked to the center of the ring and grabbed the long-armed glove. She handed it to Shane, who put it on and repeated the exercise they had done a few days earlier.

"Sit," he commanded, swinging his hand palm up to reinforce the nonverbal command.

Decoy immediately responded and he rewarded him with a treat from his non-gloved hand.

But immediately after that, he shoved his gloved hand against Decoy's nose and said, "Attack." Decoy reared back and didn't engage. He repeated the exercise, antagonizing Decoy over and over again, until Decoy finally snapped at him. But even then, it was half-hearted.

"Good boy, Decoy," Piper said, stepping in to offer Decoy a treat and reinforce the attack command.

They repeated the exercise and this time it didn't take as long for Decoy to respond and latch onto the glove. "Good boy," he said and rubbed his dog's head.

Piper provided a treat and said, "Let's try it with the suit."

When she walked over and started putting it on, he said, "No way. Let me do it."

Piper shook her head vehemently. "Although dogs can turn on their owners, I doubt Decoy would attack you, even if commanded to do it."

Shane hesitated, thinking about how gentle and patient Decoy was generally. "I'm not sure he'll attack you either."

Piper shrugged, or at least he thought she did beneath the bulk of the padded suit. "We can try," she said and motioned for him to give her the long-armed glove.

He did as she instructed, as obedient as Decoy, he realized with a strangled laugh. In more ways than she knew, Piper had him wrapped around her little finger.

He helped her put the glove on over the padded sleeve of the suit. As he had before, she instructed Decoy to sit and then antagonized the dog while giving the "Attack" command. It took even longer for Decoy to respond and even then it was clearly a half-hearted bite on the glove.

They attempted the exercise a few more times, but with little improvement.

After the last attempt, Piper shook her head and laughed. "I guess Decoy is more of a lover than a fighter."

That laugh hit him as it always did, as hard as a sucker punch to the gut, and when combined with her words, his mind spun with unwanted images of what it would be like to make love to her. Passion rose and he battled it back, laughed as she had done and in a rough voice said, "I guess he is."

Piper's green gaze darkened, picking up on his tension. "I guess," she said in barely a whisper.

He imagined that whisper as she lay in bed beside him. Voice still rough, he said, "Maybe it's time for hide-and-seek."

"Definitely," Piper said and turned away from him to remove the padded suit, almost as if by taking it off she was revealing too much. After she had put it away, she walked back to the center of the ring, arms wrapped around herself in that defensive gesture he had seen on their first day together.

With a jerky motion, she gestured to the door of the ring. "I'm going to go get some hot dogs."

She raced out of the room, leaving Shane alone with Decoy. He bent to rub the dog's ears and Decoy lapped it up, laying his paws on Shane's shoulders so he could lick at his face. "I love you, too, boy," he said, glad they were done with the protect and attack since he hated antagonizing his friend.

Decoy sat back down, but his ears perked up at the soft sound of a footstep on the floor of the training ring.

Piper was back.

He rose, his gaze fixed on her face. Such an expressive face, giving away that she was as bothered by him as he was by her. A stain of pink colored her cheeks, and she was fidgety, her hands unsure against the plastic of the hot dog bag.

He walked over, laid his hands over hers, the gesture meant to soothe, but it did anything but that. It was like being struck by lightning as awareness jolted him where their hands touched.

She sucked in a breath, and he barely had time to grab the hot dogs as she let go of the bag and stepped away.

## Chapter Eight

Piper's heart skittered in her chest in recognition of his touch and all that rampant masculinity. No matter how hard she had tried to ignore her attraction to him over the last two weeks, it had proved impossible.

She was aware of him on every level. His strength. His patience. His discipline.

But she knew that his discipline would take him from her soon. In a little over two weeks, he'd be leaving, and she had to remember that.

"This," she said and gestured with a finger between them. "It can't be more than this," she said and motioned to the training ring around them and to Decoy.

His hands tightened on the bag, clearly on edge, but then he said, "You're right. We should get back to training."

The words stuck in her throat, but she got them out somehow. "You're right."

Pointing to the edges of the structure, she said, "We have small niches all here and there in the cinder block. We'll put the hot dogs there as well as some toys."

He walked to the wall of the ring, found a niche

and put half a dog inside. As he bent to do so, his hand shook, and he let out a little gasp.

"You okay?" she asked as he straightened and rubbed his shoulder.

"I am," he said with a grimace. "I just never know when it will act up."

She'd told herself not to ask more than once when she'd seen that tell that said he was in pain. This time she couldn't hold back. "Is that why... Is it why you left the Army?"

His face was that stone slab she'd seen on the first day, but then he shook his head, looked away and expelled a harsh breath. "It is. When the IED exploded and the building came down, shrapnel tore through my shoulder. Damaged it so bad I couldn't hold a weapon with any precision. I guess I could have stayed stateside manning a desk chair, but I couldn't picture myself doing that. I had my twenty in and decided it was time to do something else."

"Like join a search and rescue group," she said as they moved on to the next little niche and she shoved in a toy that Decoy had taken a liking to in earlier sessions.

Shane shrugged, grimaced and rubbed the shoulder, but he pressed on to another of the niches and stuffed in the rest of the hot dog. "Actually, I didn't really know what I'd do, you know?"

She did. After David had died, she'd had no idea what to do. Besides taking things one day at a time. She'd been a walking zombie, just going through the paces of life until Emma and the DCA had given her new purpose. And a new life.

"I do know. If it wasn't for Emma and the DCA…" She didn't want to think about what might have been.

He turned and cupped her cheek. Wiped away the tear that had slipped down her face.

"You were meant for this, Piper. You're so good at what you do," he said.

His touch was gentle but wrapped in strength. She stepped into that strength, burying her head against his chest. Breathing out a shaky breath as he wrapped his arms around her and held her, comforting her.

Sensing the upset, Decoy sidled up to her and rubbed his head against her leg, trying to soothe her in the only way he knew how.

"Thank you, Decoy," she said and rubbed his head.

When she stepped back, she peered up at Shane and cradled his jaw. "Thank you."

He smiled, a ghost of a smile that she traced with a finger. "I should say thanks as well. The last two weeks…" He jerked his gaze away from her as he said, "Gonzo was right when he said this might be a new life for me."

But that new life would take him to a group in Montana, she reminded herself and took another step back from him. Distance would keep her from making a mistake that would only bring pain when he left.

"Which means it's time to get back to work."

THE SUN PEEKED out from the clouds just as they headed outside to go home after their training sessions.

"See you tomorrow," Piper said and picked up Chipper to put her in the car and secure her into the seat with a harness.

"See you," he said, but wasn't sure just how accurate that was since he planned to go in and speak to Emma about changing his training as soon as Piper drove away.

He waited, rocking back and forth on his heels, the soft rain-soaked ground giving beneath his feet. When her vehicle was out of view down the long drive, he pivoted and walked toward Emma's office, fully intending to ask for Emma to finish his training.

But with each step that he took, hesitation crept in.

He enjoyed working with Piper.

*You mean being with Piper*, the little voice intruded.

*Yes, being with Piper*, he admitted, as much as he didn't want to.

He pushed forward, knowing that he had to do it since it was what was best for both of them. But in his head, he heard Gonzo's voice this time, warning him not to be a fool. Not to throw away a good thing.

Which had him turning around and heading toward his pickup. His motion was so sudden that he almost tripped over Decoy, who was stuck on him like a fly on a glue trap.

He bent to rub the dog's floppy ears. "I'm so sorry, boy. It's just so confusing."

Decoy barked and looked down the drive in the direction that Piper had gone as if to also tell him not to let her go.

"Not you, too, boy," he said, shaking his head.

Decoy barked and once again peered at the driveway.

"Damn it," Shane said, but instead of heading toward his car, he walked toward the DCA offices.

THE SECOND PIPER set Chipper on the ground, the little pup strained on her leash, obviously intrigued by something on the ground.

A second later, she noticed the pup sniffing around the cigarette butt sitting at the top of her driveway, right near the path to her front door.

She pulled Chipper tight to her and thought about bundling her back into the car to return to the DCA, but she was no coward.

She also didn't want to be one of those too-stupid-to-live heroines in those slasher movies. She opened her car door, reached back into the glove compartment and took out the pepper spray she kept there. With that in hand, she approached her front door, but everything seemed in order.

The door was locked, and with a quick look around, she opened it and entered, shutting and locking it behind her quickly.

Nothing seemed amiss inside.

She slowly walked through her home, but everything was in order until she got to the sliding doors to her deck. Several muddy footprints dirtied the deck close to the doors and several of them led to the edge of the wood. Beyond the deck was a trail of trampled grass leading toward the stand of trees along the edges of the meadow.

She had no doubt someone had been there, and they hadn't been up to anything good.

Shaking, she grabbed her phone and dialed Emma.

"ARE YOU SURE this is what you want?" Emma asked, fingers steepled in front of her face as she considered Shane across the width of her desk.

"No," he answered honestly because he wasn't sure. "But it might be what's best."

Emma sucked in a deep breath. Paused before she released it. "What if I'm not sure that's what's best?"

Emma knew Piper better than anyone, he suspected. He also suspected that Emma would do whatever she needed to in order to protect her friend. Her hesitation made him wonder, but he didn't have time to ask since Emma's phone started vibrating angrily on the surface of her desk.

It was only a quick look, but he could see that it was Piper calling. He wondered if it was about the same thing he was discussing with Emma. Only as Piper's voice spilled from the phone, her words clipped and a little too loud, he knew it was about something bad.

"Did you call the police?"

"No," he heard over the line and then her words grew too garbled to understand.

"Stay inside until I get there. I'll just be a few minutes," Emma said and jumped out of her chair.

"What's wrong?" he said, following Emma as she rushed out of the building and to her car.

She stopped by her car bumper and said, "Piper thinks someone tried to break into her house."

Fear gripped his gut, and his insides went cold. "She's okay, right?"

Emma nodded. "She is. Whoever did it is long gone, but she doesn't want to call the police and bother them if it was nothing."

"Let's go, then," he said, then walked to the passenger door and grabbed the handle.

Emma looked at his hand, then at him, and her blue-eyed gaze narrowed. But with a nod, she said, "Let's go."

Once they were seated, Emma tore down the driveway, the car kicking up gravel and dirt in their haste to reach Piper.

Piper's red Jeep Rubicon was in the drive. Piper was standing by the front window, looking out for them when they pulled up. Seconds later, the front door opened, and Piper and Chipper were standing there.

She had her arms wrapped around herself, pulling a hand away only long enough for her to rake back the long strands of her red hair in obvious frustration.

In no time, they had rushed out of the car and to the door. Piper and Emma shared a tight embrace, but as he neared, Piper moved away to let him enter.

"You didn't need to come," she said, meeting his gaze.

With the arch of a brow in condemnation, he said, "You think I'd let two unarmed women face a possible burglar on their own?"

She pointed to the sliding doors, where Emma stood peering out. "If it was a burglar, he's not here anymore."

Piper walked to stand beside Emma, and he followed. At the door, both dogs seemed to scent something around the edges of the door. Decoy began to scratch there, and Chipper mimicked his actions.

"Sit," Piper and Shane said at the same time.

The dogs complied, but it was clear they wanted to go back to the door and smell some more.

As he looked out at the footprints and the flattened path of grass through the meadow toward the trees, it seemed as if whoever had been at the back door was clearly gone. But he wasn't going to take any chances.

"I'm going to check outside," he said and signaled to Decoy to come with him. He hurried back to the front door, exited and walked around the side of the house. There were no footprints there, but he could see where the grass had been flattened by someone's passage. Carefully making his way around so as to not disturb any evidence in case there was a sign of an attempted break-in, he went to the back of the house and the small wooden deck by the sliding glass doors.

Someone had been there, judging from the muddy footprints. Cautious once more not to disturb the footprints, he got on the deck and examined the jamb of the door, while inside Piper and Emma stood looking at him.

There were a few scratches near one side, but they weren't deep enough to indicate that someone had tried to jimmy the door open. Trying the door, he found it was still locked, so whoever it was had not broken the mechanism on the door.

Motioning to the handle, he said, "Please open the door."

Piper went over, flipped the lock and slid the door aside so he could enter. As he did so, he said, "Someone was clearly back here, but it's hard to tell if they tried to break in. There are some scratches by the jamb near the lock, but I'm not sure if they aren't from regular wear and tear."

"I guess there's no reason to call the police," Piper said, a combination of dejection and worry in her tone.

"There is a reason, Piper. This isn't the first thing that's happened," Shane said, prompting Emma to stare at Piper in surprise.

"This isn't the first thing?" Emma said, her voice rising in harsh question.

Piper raked back her hair with her fingers and sighed. "I didn't want to worry you and we just figured it was kids or something."

"Like what?" Emma said, peering nervously from him to Piper, who seemed to be in avoidance mode, whether it was because she was in denial about what was happening or feeling stupid that she hadn't said something to her friend.

Shane raised his hands and motioned in a calm-down gesture. "Small things, but maybe Piper should tell you and let you be the judge."

THE LAST THING Piper wanted to do was distress Emma, who had enough on her plate what with worrying about Chief Walters's possible retirement and how that would impact the DCA. Sharing the info now would hopefully prevent that worrying.

"It was just some small things. I smelled cigarette smoke one night when I came back home and felt like someone was watching me. Then someone messed with the pots by the front door, like they were looking for a key. But then nothing all of last week. Yesterday my car door was ajar—"

"You didn't mention that," Shane said, lips tight with concern and possibly anger.

"I just figured I didn't close it right. Tonight, there was a cigarette butt by the driveway that Chipper found. That's what had me looking around."

"And you noticed those footprints by your sliding doors," Emma finished for her and walked to do her own inspection of the jamb.

With a shrug, Emma said, "Shane's right about the scratches, but why was someone back there? Maybe you got home when they were about to break in, and they hightailed it out of here before you spotted them."

"Maybe, but why me? Why my house?" Piper said, worried about the various small incidents that seemed to be building toward something bigger.

Shane laid a hand on her shoulder and offered a reassuring squeeze. "It's a nice house with very little nearby. Leaving all this proof that they were here, it's an amateur thing. Maybe kids like we first thought," he said, clearly trying to make her feel more comfortable about what had happened.

"Maybe, but maybe it's time to take this a little more seriously," Emma said and whipped out her cell phone.

Piper had no doubt whom Emma was calling, which was confirmed as she said, "Hi, Chief. I hope I'm not disturbing your dinner. Can I put you on speaker?"

Since his wife had died many years earlier, the chief regularly had his dinner promptly at six at Millard's Diner. That was confirmed by the sounds of muted talking and cutlery clinking as Emma engaged the speaker function.

"You're never a bother, Emma. Theresa says hi, by the way," the chief said.

"Hi, Theresa," Emma replied.

Theresa was the secretary for Jasper PD and like a mother hen to them all. She regularly brought in home-made cupcakes and cookies for the chief and all the other officers. She knew everything about everyone in Jasper, and if you asked Piper, she had a thing for the chief, whom she flirted with regularly.

And now she was having dinner with him. *Interesting*, Piper thought, happy that maybe the chief and Theresa were a thing.

"Piper's had a few things happen around her house and we're hoping you can help," Emma said and jerked her head up, encouraging Piper to speak.

Piper shared what she had told Emma earlier and Chief Walters harrumphed and said, "Sounds like kids to me, but there's no reason to take any chances. I'll call Cal Hoover and ask him to have the men do some extra patrols in your area."

"Thanks, Chief. That would really make me feel better," Piper said. She liked the chief's third-in-command, who was an honest and dedicated man. Much like the chief, he supported the DCA's programs and Emma had helped train Cal's K-9, Ruby, a German shepherd.

"Anything for my girls," the chief said, earning a teasing, "They're not girls, Doug. They're grown women."

"Right as always, Theresa," he said with a laugh and Theresa's full-throated laugh chased the chief's.

"Thank you both. Enjoy your dinner," Emma said, then ended the call and slipped the phone back into her jeans pocket. Hands on hips, Emma gazed from her to Shane and said, "Speaking of dinner, how about some burgers and beer at Bartwell's?"

She knew Emma was only trying to put them all at ease about what had happened, and it was dinnertime after all. "I'm game. Shane?" she said, tentative about whether he would agree given what had happened earlier that day in the training ring.

With a tight smile he said, "I'm game."

## Chapter Nine

Unlike the last time they'd been in Bartwell's, there was no emergency call to pull Emma away and Shane was grateful for that. She was an excellent buffer and the laughter and conversation between the two women during dinner had helped put Piper at ease over what had happened at her home.

It also helped that as they neared her house after dinner, a Jasper PD patrol car with Officers Callan and Nichols was driving by, searchlight trained on Piper's home. After they pulled into Piper's driveway, the officers parked their cruiser and came over to greet them.

"Evening," Ava said with a tight smile. Although she had gotten friendlier over the last two weeks, she could still be standoffish at times.

"Thanks for coming by, Ava. Brady," Piper said.

Brady nodded. "We got the call from Jenny the dispatcher that Lieutenant Hoover wanted us to do some extra patrols because you were having some problems."

"Want us to look around?" Ava said and gestured with her flashlight to the house.

Piper wrapped her arms around herself and shrugged.

"I'm not sure that's necessary. Maybe I'm just overre-acting."

Ava and Brady shared that kind of cop look that Shane recognized well. They intended to look around whether or not Piper wanted it to happen. That was confirmed when Brady said, "If you don't mind, we'll just do a quick check."

They didn't wait for Piper's approval. Both officers headed off around one side of the house.

Emma laid a comforting hand on Piper's shoulder. "I'm sure everything is okay," Emma said, her tone soothing.

"I hope so," Piper said and gazed at him, as if seek-ing his reassurance.

"It doesn't hurt to take precautions. Like I said two weeks ago, maybe you should get one of those cameras and a security system."

"Maybe," Piper said, but he could tell she wasn't to-tally convinced.

Moments later the two officers came around the op-posite side of the house and returned to where they waited by Emma's car.

"Nothing, unless you count Decoy and Chipper play-ing by your sliding doors," Brady said with a smile.

"Thank you," Piper replied.

"Just to be sure, we will come by again on our pa-trols. We have had some complaints about stealing items from cars, so make sure you keep them locked. Same thing with all your windows and doors. No sense invit-ing trouble," Ava advised.

"Will do," Shane said, and with that, the two officers went back to their patrol car and took off.

Emma rubbed Piper's back. "See, no reason to worry. Ava and Brady will be popping by, but maybe I should stay tonight if that would make you feel better."

"It would, that is if you don't mind," Piper said, peering at her best friend hopefully.

"I don't. I'll just run Shane and Decoy back to his car and pick up a few things."

"See you later. Shane, thanks for everything," Piper said.

He wanted to say he hadn't done much of anything, but hopefully what he had done had helped to calm her. "Anytime, Piper. I'll see you tomorrow for training."

She nodded and bit her lip, as if to stop herself from saying anything else.

Piper opened the door and called out to Decoy, who came rushing over, Chipper tagging along behind him. He whistled to the dog to come and when he did, they walked with Emma back to her car and in minutes they were at the DCA. But once Emma had parked, she hesitated, hands gripping the wheel.

"You and Piper okay now?" she said and stared at him intently.

It made him feel like one of the dogs she was trying to control, and he didn't like it one bit. But he understood it was only because she was worried about her friend, so he tamped down his alpha response to the challenge in her tone and posture.

"She's a good trainer. We're making a lot of progress," he answered, but Emma only shook her head at that.

"Don't try and kid me, Shane. Anyone can see there's

more going on, which is why you were in my office earlier."

He shook his head. "It was, but I can handle it, especially now that she doesn't need any more upset. Piper needs someone who will be there for her. I'm not that guy for the future, but I will be for now."

Her gaze narrowed and she searched his features in the light from a spotlight trained on the parking area. With a shake of her head, she said, "I think you truly believe that, but I'm not so sure that's right. Just don't hurt her. She's been hurt enough already."

He understood. Losing a spouse, especially at such a young age, could be devastating. That Piper was handling it as well as it seemed was truly a testament to the strength of her character.

"I won't." He opened his door and let Decoy out of the back seat. Once they were in his pickup, he waited for Emma to enter her own home before driving away.

He slowed as he approached Piper's house and noticed her standing by the front window, probably waiting for Emma to come by. He waved at her, and she waved back. Then he drove away, but knew he'd be returning tonight.

While he trusted Jasper PD to be true to their word, he wasn't about to take any chances with Piper.

Despite what he'd said to Emma, he did already care for her more than was wise. Because of that, he'd do whatever was necessary to keep her safe.

"It's going to be a long night, Decoy," he said and rubbed his dog's floppy ears.

Decoy barked and licked Shane's hand, as if to confirm he was up for it.

Shane had no doubt about it. Decoy had tagged after him on a mission more than once in Afghanistan.

Only none of those missions were as important as this one. Because of that, he didn't intend to fail.

HE TRAINED THE binoculars on the comings and goings at Piper's house.

The on-and-off heavy rains had kept him from trying to get into her house all day. Once the sun had broken through, he'd raced down to her house. He'd been trying to enter through the sliding doors when he'd heard her pull up and had to make a dash for the nearby woods to hide.

He'd waited for the three of them to leave. The Three Musketeers he'd dubbed them. Emma, Piper and Shane, who would clearly be trouble.

When they'd driven off earlier that night, probably for dinner, he'd intended to go back and finish the job, only it had become like Grand Central Station down there.

First the cops had driven by. Then the Three Musketeers had shown up. Then it had been just Piper, but before he could act, Shane had come by in his red pickup. Barely minutes later, Emma had pulled up and gone into the house.

He could probably handle Piper and her annoying little dog. But restraining two strong women would definitely be a problem.

He'd have to wait, but not too long. He couldn't keep on doing petty thefts around town because they were already attracting too much attention. The tip jars were being watched more closely and people had started to lock their cars and doors in a town where people normally didn't do things like that.

Just another few days and he'd go in, no matter what it took. No matter what happened afterward.

He couldn't wait any longer to take what was rightfully his.

THE TENSION THAT had erupted between them in the training ring had been replaced by worry over the possible break-in at her house.

But Emma staying over that night as well as the very obvious police patrols by her home had alleviated her concerns somewhat. So had Shane's nighttime visits over the last two days. She had caught him twice when she'd been unable to sleep and had gone to her living room to watch some late-night television.

She'd waved at him and he at her, but neither had acknowledged his patrols during their training the last two days. They were all focused on Decoy and the excellent progress he was making with their search and rescue training.

"Good boy," she said, then patted his head and offered up a treat for his finding one of the toys in the indoor training area.

"He is doing well," Shane said with a smile and likewise rubbed Decoy's head, but as he did so, his hand grazed hers and they both pulled back at the instant zing of awareness.

"He is," she said and tucked her hands under her arms. "It's a beautiful day out there. Maybe we should take him out on the trail today."

"I think Decoy would like that," he said, then awkwardly added, "I would, too."

"Great. Let me round up some hot dogs and get them set up on the trail," she said.

"I'll go with you," he said, but she shook her head.

"I don't want Decoy to see where I put the food. Why don't you get yourself a coffee and a doughnut and wait for me in Emma's office. I think she took one of the horses out for a ride today."

ALTHOUGH NOTHING HAD happened in the last two days besides long stretches of heavy rain, Shane felt uneasy about letting Piper go out on the trail alone. But he wasn't sure Piper would appreciate him being overprotective.

With a nod, Shane said, "I'll skip the doughnut, but coffee sounds great."

Piper eyed him up and down and grinned. "Watching your girlish figure?"

Shane laughed and shook his head. More like he was watching hers, but he laid a hand on his flat midsection and said, "Can't let this go to flab."

Her gaze dropped to his hand and that flush that was becoming all too familiar blossomed across her face. "I'll get the dogs and set up the trail."

She rushed out of the indoor ring, and he followed more slowly to give her space. In the hallway, she went to a small refrigerator where they kept the hot dogs as well as their lunches and snacks while he ambled to the coffee station and poured himself a cup.

Piper raced out the door with the dogs, but instead

of heading to Emma's office, he walked Decoy outside and to the far corner of the building.

"Sit," he commanded, and Decoy obeyed.

"Good boy." He patted him on the head and offered up a treat.

"Stay," he said and walked around the corner of the building to watch Piper out on the trail behind the barn and DCA offices. The trail ran down the length of the open meadow, but then veered off to another section of the DCA's nearly twenty acres.

He sipped and watched, keeping an eye on her as long as he could. Counting the minutes until she had doubled back and came into view once more. She caught sight of him as he stood there and shook her head, as if chastising him, but smiled.

The smile warmed his insides as powerfully as the rays of the spring sun beating down on him.

He finished his coffee and waited for her to return. Once she got there, she flipped a hand in the direction of the door to the offices. "Let me just get Chipper from her crate. I'm sure she'd love to walk with us."

"Sure thing. Decoy loves Chipper," he said.

The dog's ears perked up at the mention of the puppy's name, dragging a laugh from both of them.

"The feeling's mutual," Piper said and hurried into the building. She returned with Chipper, tail wagging and a smile plastered on her face. The puppy immediately raced to Decoy's side and climbed all over the older dog. Decoy laid a big paw on Chipper's head and playfully tussled with her.

"I hope Decoy won't be distracted," Shane said and gave a hand command for Decoy to come to his side.

"It'll be a good test to see if he can stay focused," Piper said and started walking toward the trail, Chipper on the leash beside her, almost prancing.

Decoy was more reserved as they followed until they were on the trail. Then they walked side by side for a few yards until Piper said, "Search, Decoy. Search, boy."

Decoy immediately started nosing at the underbrush along the edges of the trail, much like he had done in the indoor ring. He hadn't gone more than ten feet when he nosed into the high grasses and came out with the hot dog in his mouth.

Piper went over to him and took the hot dog from his mouth. "Good boy. Bark," she said and much like he had been trained in the indoor ring, Decoy started barking, alerting them in much the same way he would hopefully do if he found a lost person.

"Good boy," she said and returned to offer Decoy the hot dog as a reward along with an enthusiastic rub of his head and sides.

When she was done, Piper faced him and said, "It's your turn."

He nodded and led Decoy forward on the path. "Search, Decoy."

As he had before, Decoy nosed all along the edges of the underbrush, shifting from one side of the trail to the other until about ten yards ahead, he stopped at the edge of the trail. Decoy buried his nose in some tall grasses and then emerged with one of his favorite toys in his mouth. He dropped it on the ground and did a short quick bark.

"Tell him to bark again," Piper said.

He did and Decoy tilted his head to the side and peered at him with a seemingly puzzled look.

"Bark," he repeated, but had to do it a second time for Decoy to finally obey.

"Good boy," he said and offered up a reward again, reinforcing the behavior.

They repeated the exercise, strolling slowly along the trail, Chipper occasionally engaging Decoy in play that was short-lived since Decoy almost intuitively knew what they were doing wasn't a game.

With the weather as nice as it was, the training was pleasant, especially since Decoy caught on quickly, earning more treats than admonishments to search or bark.

"He's doing so well. You'll be further ahead than most when you finish your lessons and go to that search and rescue group," she said, but bit her lip as soon as she said it.

"He is doing well," Shane said and tried to ignore the fact that their time together would soon come to a close, much as she had said.

But no matter how hard both of them tried to ignore it, the reality that their lessons would soon be over cast a pall over the rest of their walk. By the time they reached the end of the trail, the sun had started to drop along the horizon.

"I didn't realize how late it was," she said and instructed Chipper to turn back in the direction of the barn and DCA offices.

Shane gazed up at the afternoon sky and nodded. "It'll be dark soon. I didn't see your Jeep in the parking spaces."

"I walked," she said with a shrug.

Shane arched a brow and she looked away to avoid the reproach in his gaze. "It might be dark for your walk home."

Piper shot a fleeting look at the night sky. "It might."

Frustrated, he said, "It may not be safe for you to walk it alone."

Piper gestured to Chipper. "I have Chipper, and honestly, nothing has happened in the last few days. Plus, I can go from here and it'll be a short walk."

He couldn't argue with that. "You're right, but there are still bears, foxes and mountain lions."

"Lions, and tigers and bears, oh my!" she teased, but then nodded. "There are, but I haven't seen any scat or other signs of predators in the area."

She was being difficult, but he wasn't about to let her walk home in the dark.

"I'll go with you."

"You don't have to," she protested, glancing at him from the corner of her eye.

"I'll go," he said, and his tone brooked no disagreement.

Apparently realizing that, she nodded. "Okay, but I'm sure it's not necessary."

He did a quick lift of his shoulders in agreement but pressed on. "I'm sure you're right, but why take chances?"

As he said the words, he realized they could refer to more than just the walk to her home. Being with her, even for something as short as a five-minute stroll, made him wonder about what it would be like not to leave when the lessons were over. That was a dangerous thing, and as she lifted her gaze to meet his, he liked to think she was feeling the same way. As if it was too soon for him to leave, but he hadn't planned on staying.

He hadn't planned on meeting someone like Piper either, for that matter.

That she felt the same was confirmed as she said, "It's just a quick walk home."

"That it is," he said with a determined nod.

But as he ambled with her and Chipper across a break in the trail and the meadow, the tension built between them, warning him that it was about much, much more.

# Chapter Ten

The sun hadn't been enough to dry out some large sections of the meadow. They had to slog through inch-deep pools of water, and in other areas, their feet sank deep into the ground.

"It was a lot drier by the DCA. I'm sorry," Piper said as she lifted her booted foot from a muddy patch with a sucking sound.

"You couldn't have known," he said and pointed toward one section of the meadow. "Can't we walk straight through there to the road?"

From beside him, Piper ran her gaze down the length of his arm to where he aimed. "We can. Even though it's a little longer, it might make more sense to cut over and walk along the road. It's got to be drier."

"Let's go, then," he said and took the first step, but when she went to follow him, the unsteady ground made her lose her balance.

Shane reached out to hold her arm and provide support. "Thanks."

He nodded, kept his grip on her while she pulled her foot from the mud and stepped onto steadier ground.

When she took another steadier step, he looped his arm through hers and she didn't protest.

The feel of his arm tucked through hers, the slight weight of his body as it brushed against her as they walked, was comforting.

Too comforting. It would be too easy to get used to having him beside her every day. She hadn't expected that. If anything, she had worried that his being military would be a too-painful reminder of David.

*David*, she thought, and guilt swept through her. She'd loved David with all her heart. She'd grieved deeply over his death. Hadn't ever thought about being attracted to another man, especially a military man.

But she was also sure David wouldn't have wanted her to be alone for the rest of her life.

She gazed up at Shane, at his strong profile, all hard lines and angles until he looked down and smiled at her. Then his features softened and his blue eyes, bright as an Idaho spring day, glittered when he met her gaze.

"You okay?" he asked, his eyes narrowing slightly.

She didn't hesitate to say, "I'm okay."

With a quick nod, they pushed on in deep dusk, shadows surrounding them as they walked along the road. But as they passed a dense stand of trees a few yards from her house, she caught sight of a blue pickup sitting in front of her home which was all lit up even though she didn't remember leaving the lights on.

But even with the lights on, it was impossible to see who was at the wheel, especially as the headlights snapped on, blinding her.

A split second later, the pickup screeched toward them, so close that Shane had to jerk her away to keep her from being hit.

"WHAT THE HELL?" Shane said, mumbled a curse and tried to get a better look at the pickup, but it was too dark and quickly too far away.

"Did you get the plate number?" Piper asked and rubbed her hands along her arms.

He shook his head. "I couldn't."

"I didn't either. I was too scared," Piper said and took a step toward her home, but he shot out a hand to stop her.

She looked up at him, puzzled. "What's wrong?"

"He was in front of your house, Piper. You don't recognize the pickup?" Jasper was a small town, and he figured most people knew what other people drove.

She shook her head. "No. I mean, there are a couple of other blue pickups only..."

He detected the unease that crept into her voice as it trailed off. "But you didn't recognize that one. You didn't see the driver?"

She once again shook her head. "No."

"Me either." It had been too dark, and the sudden snap of the headlights had blinded him.

He peered toward Piper's house, worried that whoever was driving the pickup hadn't been there for a good reason. With a reluctant nod, he said, "I guess we should go."

"We should," Piper said, but he took the lead, walking ahead of her toward the front door.

At the sight of it, they both stopped short.

The door was wide open and hanging off the hinges. Lights were on inside the house, and he could see couch pillows, papers and other objects on the living room floor.

Chipper immediately started barking and Decoy's ears perked up and he joined in the chorus, adding his deeper bark.

"Quiet," Piper commanded and both dogs stopped, sensing the urgency in her voice.

Piper walked toward the front door, but he once again stopped her with a gentle touch on her arm.

"Let me go first. We don't know if someone is still in there."

Eyes wide, pupils dilated with fear, she slowly dipped her head and said, "Don't touch anything. Just in case we have to call the police."

Shane had no doubt they would have to call the police because he was certain they were entering a crime scene. He grabbed the leashes for the two dogs from her and tied them to a post at the alcove by the front door. Striding to the open door, he paused in the entryway, examining the destruction inside the house. Piper pushed at his back, wanting to get past him, and he slowly shifted to the side to let her see.

"Oh no," she said and covered her mouth with her hand. Tears gathered in her gaze, and she stumbled when she stepped past him and into the ruins of her home.

Gingerly they stepped around the strewn papers and broken bits.

"I don't understand," she said as she stood in the middle of her living room and kitchen open space, her voice choked with emotion. Tears trailing down her face.

He wrapped her up in his arms and kissed her temple. "I'm sorry, Piper."

He held her for long seconds, comforting her. Tucking her head tight against his shoulder to hide the mess around them. Although he wanted to see if the rest of the home was as bad, his first mission was to get Piper out of the house and call the police.

With her pressed tight to his side, he walked her out and she plopped down on her front stoop, arms wrapped around herself. Tears still leaked from her eyes and slipped down her face as he called 911.

When Jenny the dispatcher answered, he said, "I need to report a burglary." He provided the information to her and then turned his attention back to Piper, hunkering down in front of her. "I'm going to call Emma also."

She nodded and swiped at her tears angrily before meeting his gaze.

"Why would anyone do this?" she said and whipped a hand in the direction of her ravaged home.

"They were looking for something," he said, peering back in the direction of her front door.

"Everything of value is right out in the open. My wedding rings. Laptop. Tablet. It's all there," she said, her tone laced with anger and disbelief.

Shane shrugged, unsure of how to answer. "We'll know more once the police arrive and take a closer look around."

After a backward glance toward her home, Piper nodded.

The distant sound of a siren grew stronger as the police car approached. When the cruiser pulled up in front, the siren silenced, but the last light of dusk was broken by the red and blue of the flashing lights on the car.

Decoy sat silently by the front step, but Chipper was cowering behind him, clearly upset by the sound and lights. Shane suspected she would have run off, but the leash tied to the post had restrained her.

Officers Callan and Nichols stepped out of the car just as Emma screeched to a halt behind their cruiser.

They approached slowly while Emma ran over to Piper, who popped to her feet and embraced the other woman.

"What happened?" she said, glancing between him and the open door of Piper's home.

"Someone broke in," Piper said.

As the officers approached, Shane explained, "We were walking home and just as we got past that stand of trees," he said and pointed to the small saplings and underbrush at one edge of the property, "a blue pickup came at us. Almost ran us over."

Ava and Brady shared a look and Ava took a small notebook and pen from her jacket pocket. "Did you get a license plate number?"

Piper shook her head. "The headlights were too bright and it all happened so fast."

Ava laid a reassuring hand on Piper's arm. "It's okay, Piper. Could you tell the make?"

She shook her head. "No. Just a pickup."

Brady nodded. "Let us go inside and take a look around. See if there's any evidence."

With a jerk of his head in the direction of the door,

Ava and Brady walked inside while Piper, Emma and Shane waited outside.

Long, almost painful minutes passed before Ava and Brady came back out. They once again shared a look that brought no comfort to Shane. If anything, it brought more worry about what was happening.

"What's up?" he asked, certain he wouldn't like what he was about to hear.

"We need you to come with us. Take a look around," Ava said to Piper, her tone soothing while at the same time in command.

"Okay," Piper said, voice weak. Emma had her arm around Piper's shoulder and together the two of them followed the officers into the home, Shane trailing after them.

Foam guts spilled from the slashes in the sofa pillows and cushions. Every drawer in a nearby desk was yanked open, the contents spilled all over the floor. Books and bric-a-brac torn from a nearby bookshelf joined the mess on the floor.

In the kitchen area, cabinet doors were thrown open, one so violently the hinge was torn from the cabinet body. Plates had been jerked from the cabinets, but luckily not all of them were broken. The fridge door was ajar, as if they had also searched inside.

"I don't get it," Piper said, gesturing to the laptop that still sat on her desk and a tablet on the floor by an overturned coffee table.

"They were looking for something specific," Ava said. "Can you think of what that might be?"

Piper shook her head.

Together they all approached the guest bedroom and

Piper went in with the officers to look. There was similar destruction, but apparently nothing seemed to have been taken.

It was a different and yet similar story in Piper's bedroom. As he stood at the door watching, Piper walked around, her gaze filling with tears again, especially as she caught sight of her husband's duffel bag ripped open, his Marine uniform tossed on the floor. She went to pick it up, but Ava braced an arm across her front to keep her from touching it.

"I'm sorry, Piper. It's still evidence," she said and gestured to the contents of the room. "Is anything missing?"

ON ONE HEEL, Piper did a slow spin, looking all around the room, still reeling from the sight of David's belongings strewn on the floor.

At the sight of the empty spot on top of her dresser, her heart clenched to a stop and pain erupted in the middle of her chest. "My wedding rings are gone," she said in barely a whisper. She couldn't seem to get enough air to speak past the ache in her heart.

Emma immediately came to her side and squeezed her shoulder. "We'll find them."

"Anything else?" Ava asked, her light brown eyes filled with compassion.

Piper did another look around the room but shook her head. "Not that I can tell."

As her gaze drifted around again, it met Shane's and locked with his. It was full of compassion and caring and her heart finally began to beat again, slow, heavy beats, as if to remind her she was still alive.

"You may find something's missing once the shock wears off and you look around," Brady said with a tight smile. "But for now, it's best you stay somewhere else. You'll be safer and we need to process the house for evidence."

"You can stay with me," Emma said and rubbed her hand across Piper's shoulder.

"Thanks. I appreciate it," she said.

She took a faltering step toward the door, almost falling, her knees felt so weak. Shane was immediately there, slipping his arm around her waist to offer support. "Thanks," she said, voice as shaky as her knees.

"We've got you," Emma said, obviously forcing an upbeat note in her tone.

Once they were outside, Emma and Shane directed her toward Emma's car, but Piper pulled away from them to turn back toward her home. "I'll need some clothes."

Shane held her arms and bent slightly to force her to meet his gaze. "You can't take anything right now, Piper. Maybe tomorrow."

"I have some things that will fit you. We're almost the same size," Emma said and opened the passenger side door.

Piper looked between them and knew they were right. "Okay. Tomorrow," she said, only able to manage short responses.

SHANE HELPED PIPER ease into Emma's car and shut the door behind her.

After he finished, he stood there, Emma in front of him. "She's in shock," he said.

Emma nodded. "I'll take care of her."

"I know you will. But if it's all right with you, I'd like to move my RV to the DCA. Stay close by just in case." He looked toward the house and said, "Let me get the dogs so you can take them now. They'll help distract Piper."

Without waiting for Emma's response, he hurried to Decoy and Chipper and untied the leashes. He walked them to Emma's car and popped them into the back seat before slipping inside as well since his pickup was still at the DCA.

It took less than five minutes to reach Emma's home. In unspoken agreement, Emma took Piper and the dogs into the house. He marched to his pickup much like he would if he'd been given a mission in the Army. His mission now: to protect Piper and find out who was responsible for terrorizing her because it was about more than a break-in.

Whoever had done this had been watching her. Doing little things to make her doubt herself. To make her worry.

He needed to find out why and he needed to make it stop.

## Chapter Eleven

In mission mode, he had his RV hitched to his pickup and was on the road to the DCA in record time.

When he reached Emma's, he parked his RV on a flat area where he had seen Emma occasionally park a horse trailer. As he stepped from the pickup and walked toward the house, Emma's front door opened and she stood there, silhouette limned by the light from inside.

She walked onto the porch, careful not to let the screen door bang behind her.

He jerked his chin in the direction of her house. "How's Piper doing?"

Emma crossed her arms and did a half glance toward the door. "Freaked out. I had her take a hot shower and change into pajamas. She's in bed and the dogs are in the room with her. I think they know she needs the company."

Shane was sure that Decoy sensed it. More than once his dog had climbed into bed to comfort him when Shane was having a nightmare.

"Can I see her?" he asked.

Emma dipped her head to confirm it. "Guest room is down the hall."

Shane didn't hesitate. He marched into the house and down the hall to where Piper was lying in bed, the two dogs stretched out on the floor beside her.

She sat up when she saw him, and the two dogs perked up and peered in his direction.

"How are you feeling?" he said and sat beside her, Decoy and Chipper rearranging themselves at his feet.

"BETTER," SHE SAID, and it was the truth.

When she'd first gotten into the shower, her insides had felt like ice and she'd been trembling from the shock of what had happened. The warm shower had helped chase away the chill, and little by little, she'd been able to stop shaking.

"We're going to find out who did this," Shane said and laid his hand over hers. Twined his fingers with hers. "In the meantime, you'll stay with Emma until we can fix your place up and get a security system in place. I'll be right outside in the RV."

"You don't have to do that. Emma has a security system and maybe it was just a simple break-in. There have been others in town, I think," she said, trying to convince herself that's what it had been.

Shane grimaced and shook his head. "I think it was more than that, Piper."

"But he took my wedding rings," she shot back.

With a reluctant dip of his head, he said, "He did. Hopefully you're right. In the morning, we'll see if we can set things to right at your house."

She could continue to argue with him that it wasn't necessary, but she knew he wouldn't be dissuaded. "Thanks."

"Try to get some sleep," he said and leaned forward, hesitant. Tentative as he met her gaze and brushed a quick kiss on her lips.

"Good night."

"Good night," she said to his back as he rushed from the room.

Decoy and Chipper followed him, but he commanded, "Stay."

They obeyed and returned to lie by the side of her bed.

She reached up and gently brushed her fingertips across her lips, wondering if she'd maybe imagined it, only… She hadn't. And if she was being honest with herself, she wished it would happen again, and not just the fleeting kiss from seconds ago.

"You okay?" Emma said from the doorway, brows furrowed over sky-blue eyes.

Surprisingly, she was way more okay than she'd been just moments before.

"I'm okay. Confused," she confessed, knowing Emma would understand.

"Shane?" Emma asked and leaned against the door-jamb.

"Shane," she admitted. "He's what I expected but not."

"He's changed since he got here. So have you," Emma said.

She had changed a little. So had he. But despite that, there was one truth she had to acknowledge. "He'll be gone soon."

"Maybe," Emma said and straightened. "I've set the alarm and let Tashya know what's up. She's on a date with Jason and I suggested it would be better if she stayed with him tonight."

"That might be for the best. I get the feeling it'll be wedding time for them soon anyway." Tashya and Jason had been dating for nearly four years but had grown up together as fosters in Emma's care. Now that they were both settled with good jobs, she had no doubt something more permanent would happen.

"I get that feeling also," Emma said and smiled, obviously pleased by that prospect. "I'll see you in the morning. Try to get some sleep."

With the alarm system in place as well as Emma, the dogs and Shane nearby, she'd certainly feel safe from whoever had trashed her house.

But as she slipped off to sleep, memories came again of that fleeting kiss, warning her that her heart might not be as safe.

THE NIGHTMARE CLAWED its way from his subconscious, imprisoning him in its grasp.

Heavy weight on his chest and legs, pinning him to rough, uneven ground. He called for help, but his voice was weak, his throat dry. Dirt rained down on him from above, threatening to choke him. He drew in an agonized breath, and something rattled in his chest.

Coughing, the coppery taste of blood filled his mouth. Wet his lips.

*I'm dying*, he thought and fought to free himself from the rubble.

But as he did so, more concrete and dirt tumbled onto him, burying him alive.

He screamed and it pulled him from sleep.

He was sitting upright in bed, his body bathed in damp sweat. His muscles quivering and his heart beating so violently, he looked down to see if it was jumping out of his chest.

Sucking in a long, slow breath, he tried to restore calm in the hopes of getting back to sleep. It would take time, especially now that Decoy was inside with Piper. The dog's presence not only helped after a nightmare, but it also often kept them away.

But not tonight. Tonight, he'd just have to tough it out.

It took long hours before he slipped off to a light sleep that didn't last for long as the first fingers of light crept past the edges of the blinds to warn that morning had arrived.

He washed and dressed quickly. Made himself a cup of coffee for some energy and hurried out, determined to put things to right at Piper's home as soon as possible.

There were no lights on in Emma's home as he left his RV and climbed into his pickup for the drive into Jasper, where he intended to pick up an off-the-shelf security system, doorbell camera, wood to repair her jamb and new hinges for the door.

But before he hit any of the stores in town for the supplies, he dropped by the headquarters for Jasper PD.

The one-story green-and-white building was located on West Main Street, just off the town square. He parked in front and walked through the large glass front doors and into a reception area and waiting room. A young Asian woman sat behind the reception desk, taking calls, and he remembered her from their visit to the brewery the other day.

As he came up to the desk, Jenny raised a finger to indicate she'd be with him as soon as she finished the call.

He examined the station as he waited. Behind the desk were doors to an open room with desks and two offices. Two officers were sitting at their desks, but he didn't recognize them.

At the far end of the room was what appeared to be a large meeting room and a break room where he spied a coffee maker, refrigerator and microwave. To the left of the reception area were four holding cells and two rooms, probably for interviews, he guessed. The furniture was a little dated, and the paint was that indeterminate institutional color that could be either gray or blue. However, the space was brightly lit, neat, clean and orderly.

As he waited, an older woman walked through the front doors carrying in a plastic-wrapped dish holding what looked like pound cake. She had short gray hair and bright blue eyes. He guessed she was in her late fifties, sixty at most, and a bit matronly.

When she saw him, she smiled and said, "May I help you?"

He nodded and held out his hand. "Shane Adler. I was hoping to speak to someone about the break-in at Piper Lambert's home."

The older woman shook his hand and arched a brow. "Theresa Norwood. I'm Chief Walters's secretary. Are you a friend of Piper's?"

"I am. I was with her last night when it happened," he explained.

Jenny had just finished her call and piped in with,

# Treat Yourself with 2 Free Books!

**Claim up to FOUR NEW BOOKS & TWO MYSTERY GIFTS –
absolutely FREE!**

Dear Reader,

We both know life can be difficult at times. That's why it's important to treat yourself so you can relax and recharge once in a while.

And I'd like to help you do this by sending you this amazing offer of up to FOUR brand new full length FREE BOOKS that WE pay for.

**This is everything I have ready to send to you right now:**

Try **Harlequin® Romantic Suspense** books featuring heart-racing page-turners with unexpected plot twists and irresistible chemistry that will keep you guessing to the very end.

Try **Harlequin Intrigue® Larger-Print** books featuring action-packed stories that will keep you on the edge of your seat. Solve the crime and deliver justice at all costs.

Or TRY BOTH!

All we ask in return is that you answer 4 simple questions on the attached Treat Yourself survey. You'll get **Two Free Books** and **Two Mystery Gifts** from each series you try, *altogether worth over $20!* Who could pass up a deal like that?

Sincerely,

*Pam Powers*

Harlequin Reader Service

# Treat Yourself to Free Books and Free Gifts.

## Answer 4 fun questions and get rewarded.

**DETACH AND MAIL CARD TODAY!** ▶ ▶

|  | YES | NO |
|---|---|---|
| 1. I LOVE reading a good book. | ◯ | ◯ |
| 2. I indulge and "treat" myself often. | ◯ | ◯ |
| 3. I love getting FREE things. | ◯ | ◯ |
| 4. Reading is one of my favorite activities. | ◯ | ◯ |

### TREAT YOURSELF • Pick your 2 Free Books...

Yes! Please send me my Free Books from each series I select and Free Mystery Gifts. I understand that I am under no obligation to buy anything, as explained on the back of this card.

Which do you prefer?

❑ **Harlequin® Romantic Suspense** 240/340 HDL GRCZ
❑ **Harlequin Intrigue® Larger-Print** 199/399 HDL GRCZ
❑ **Try Both** 240/340 & 199/399 HDL GRDD

FIRST NAME                    LAST NAME

ADDRESS

APT.#            CITY

STATE/PROV.      ZIP/POSTAL CODE

EMAIL ❑ Please check this box if you would like to receive newsletters and promotional emails from Harlequin Enterprises ULC and its affiliates. You can unsubscribe anytime.

HI/HRS-520-TY22

"That was Ava and Brady. They just finished process-ing the house and are on their way back. They should be here soon."

"Well, then. Why don't you come in and get settled in the meeting room. I'll put up a fresh pot of coffee and you can have some of this," she said and raised the dish with the confection.

He dipped his head gratefully. "I'd appreciate that. I could use a cup of coffee and that looks delicious."

Theresa got him settled in the meeting room and he could hear her puttering about next door in the break room. In no time the earthy scent of fresh coffee per-fumed the room, and she came in with a piece of the pound cake on a small paper plate.

"Feel free to go next door and grab yourself some coffee. Milk and cream are in the fridge."

He had just finished making himself a cup when the sound of the door opening had him looking out into the open space where Ava and Brady had just entered.

They looked tired and he suspected they'd been working all night.

When Ava noticed him, she motioned to Brady and they both walked over to the meeting room.

"Good morning," he said and rose from the table.

"It could be better," Ava said.

Brady motioned for him to sit back down and added, "We could only get a couple of partial prints. Whoever it was either wiped things down or put on gloves."

"We did get some shoe prints from the floor of the living room," Ava said and pulled out her camera to show them to Shane.

Shane immediately recognized the tread. "Looks like standard-issue combat boots."

Brady nodded. "That's what I thought as well."

Ava swiped her finger across the screen to show him another set of photos. "We also have a partial tire tread. I may be a city girl, but even I can tell these belong to a truck and not a car."

"The blue pickup that nearly ran us down?" Shane asked, then sipped his coffee and broke off a piece of his pound cake.

Brady nodded. "Possibly, but don't get your hopes up too soon. This area is packed with pickups and it's likely this one was stolen. We'll be checking that out after we take a short break for breakfast."

"Thank you. Is it okay for Piper to go back home?" Shane asked and Ava nodded.

"It is, but we'd recommend a doorbell camera at a minimum. Simple security system would be better," she said.

He rose from the meeting room table and popped the last of the pound cake into his mouth. "I planned to work on all that this morning. Will you call Piper and let her know what's happening?"

"We will," Ava confirmed.

"Great. Then I'm off," he said, and after shaking hands with the two officers and thanking Theresa, he headed off to town to fetch the supplies he needed for all the repairs and improvements.

It took less than an hour to pick up what he needed and make his way back to Piper's house.

Emma's car was in front, so he suspected the two women were already inside, trying to straighten things up.

He wasn't wrong. They had already put things back into the desk drawers and onto the bookshelves. The overturned coffee table was back in place, together with the couch cushions, which had been turned slashed-side down.

As Piper noticed his attention, she said, "I'll have to get a new couch, but that'll do for now."

"Are you okay?" he asked as he set down the bags with all his purchases by the front door.

"As okay as can be expected. You didn't have to do all that," she said and gestured to the bags.

"On the contrary, I do. I'm sure you spoke to Ava or Brady, who recommended some upgrades around here."

Her lips tightened and she nodded. "They did. Thank you."

"I guess I'll get to that while you and Emma finish up," he said and started by fixing the doorjamb and hinges. He opened and closed the door several times to make sure it latched properly and, satisfied, he turned his attention to the doorbell camera and security system.

A little more than an hour later he'd wired up the camera and set up contact sensors on all the doors and windows as well as motion detectors in the common areas. He passed Piper and Emma more than once as he worked to install the system and they cleaned up the mess.

He had just finished configuring the base station that connected all the devices and kept the system online when Piper and Emma came into the living room with two garbage bags.

"Almost done," he said. To complete the installation, Piper would have to establish an online monitoring account, but even without that, any entry without disarming the system would set off a siren. That was usually enough to discourage small-time burglars.

"We're finished, so I guess it's time for me to head back and get some work done," Emma said and lugged one garbage bag out the door.

Piper followed her and they both walked to the curb to place the bags there for her usual garbage pickup.

As Shane finished checking that the keypad by the front door was securely fastened, he watched as Piper and Emma embraced. Emma ran her hand across Piper's back and up to her hair. They exchanged words that made Piper shoot a quick look in his direction and nod. And then Emma strode toward her car, got in and drove away.

Piper slowly trudged back toward the house, obviously troubled.

# Chapter Twelve

*Don't be afraid of what's happening with Shane.*

That's what Emma had said to her as they'd embraced at the curb.

Only she wasn't so much afraid as she was confused. Especially with all that was happening now.

It was just too much, and to think about any kind of relationship with Shane could only bring trouble because her emotions were too raw at the moment.

But there he was, taking care of her. Making her feel things she hadn't felt since David.

"Thank you for everything," she said and leaned a hand on the jamb, still a little unsteady with all that had happened.

"It's what…friends do," he said with a shrug that stretched the fabric of his T-shirt across his broad shoulders.

She squinted as she examined his features and said, "Is that what we are? Friends?"

Decoy and Chipper, who up until that moment had been contentedly lying together just inside the front door, hopped up and started barking.

"What's up, Decoy?" he said and stroked his head to

try to calm him, but Decoy raced out the door and toward the stand of trees on the far side of her property, Chipper following close behind.

Piper and Shane raced after the dogs, who had paused by the trees but hadn't stopped barking.

"Quiet," they both said, but had to repeat it several times until the dogs finally listened and sat down in the grass.

Piper scrutinized the area where the dogs had been barking and noticed some of the underbrush had been flattened. "There," she said and pointed to it.

Shane nodded and glanced past the matted-down underbrush to the grassy area beyond. He gestured to the area. "Looks like there are tire tracks there, but are they fresh ones?"

Fear gripped Piper at the thought the burglar had returned. Determined not to let it get to her, she pushed through the underbrush to where the tire tracks were. They led to the road and were clearly from some kind of truck. As Shane joined her, Piper said, "Do you think these could be from the pickup?"

Shane squatted to examine the tracks. "Could be."

He started to straighten but then pointed to where there were a couple of cigarette butts on the grass.

"You said you smelled cigarette smoke. He was here, watching you," Shane said, then rose and came to her side. He embraced her but she remained stiff in his arms.

"It's going to be okay. I'll bring my RV around and stay here," he said and stepped away, but quickly added, "If that's okay with you."

Shane being here would be complicated. She'd certainly feel safer from the burglar. But emotionally…

"It's okay," she said with a slow bob of her head.

"Good. Let's set up the alarm for the security system and arm it while I go get my RV. We'll call Ava and Brady as well to come inspect this area."

Her nod this time was certain. "Sounds like a plan."

WITH PIPER'S HELP, he was able to maneuver the RV into a grassy space to one side of Piper's home and set up his solar panels to power it.

He put his hands on his hips and smiled. "Looks good."

Piper nodded. "It does. Thank you again."

"It's not a problem. I need to know you're safe," Shane said. A second later, a loud rumble emanated from his midsection. He splayed a hand across his stomach and said, "I've been so busy I forgot to eat. How about you?"

She smiled and shook her head. "I didn't and I could eat a horse."

"I've heard a great deal about Millard's Diner. That is if you like it and would like to go," he said just as another deep rumble embarrassed him, bringing unwanted heat to his face.

Piper laughed and reached up to brush her thumb across his cheeks. "I love their burgers, but they have lots of wonderful daily specials."

"Great. Let's go, then," he said and slipped his arm through hers. This time she was fluid against him, leaning into his side. Smiling as he helped her into his pickup.

The ride to town was blessedly short and his hunger was quickly tamped down by his first bite of an absolutely wonderful burger. "As good as I'd heard."

Piper grinned and picked up her burger. "Glad you weren't disappointed."

"I wasn't. Just like I'm not disappointed with everything I've been learning at the DCA," he said, wanting to keep the conversation to anything other than the break-in.

"Truthfully, it's been a pleasure to work with you since Decoy has so many natural skills. The two of you will be a wonderful addition to any search and rescue team," she said and took a big bite of her burger. "Mmm, so tasty."

"There's still a lot to learn," Shane said, then snagged an onion ring and took a big bite.

With a small shake of her head, she said, "There is. Working with Decoy and you has me learning as well so I can keep on challenging you."

Shane couldn't resist teasing her. He arched a brow and said, "So I challenge you?"

A becoming flush of pink painted her cheeks. "You know you do. But I think I challenge you, too."

He chuckled and grinned, admiring her spirit. "You do. I wasn't expecting someone like you."

Around mouthful of burger, she said, "Ditto."

He barked out a laugh and started eating again, enjoying the burger and the company. It was turning out to be such a nice night, he didn't have the heart to ask anything about the burglary. There would be time enough on the drive home.

*Home...*

When he had left California and headed to Idaho, it had never occurred to him that in just a few short weeks he'd think of it as home, but there it was. Jasper felt like home. Or maybe it was more accurate to say that Piper made it feel that way.

But in a little over two weeks, he was supposed to be on his way to Montana. Away from Jasper.

Away from Piper.

His heart did a little skip at that, forcing him to suck in a breath. The air was tinged with the faint scent of something floral. Piper's soap or maybe her shampoo.

They finished dinner with a slice of Millard's cherry pie and ice cream. A perfect ending to their meal together.

But once they started their drive home, he had no choice but to ask the hard questions. He hesitated until they were almost to Piper's. Gripping the wheel tightly, he shot a quick look at her. She looked peaceful and he hated to upset that peacefulness, but it had to be done.

"Can you think of a reason why someone would be watching you? What they would want to steal from you?"

The smile that had been on her face just moments before evaporated in the blink of an eye. "Like my wedding rings?"

He hadn't wanted to say it before, but something about the theft of the wedding rings struck him as wrong.

"The rings were right there, out in the open. So were your laptop, tablet and other things someone could pawn for quick money. No reason for them to trash the house the way they did."

Piper looked down and did a little shrug. "Kids do stupid things," she said, clearly in denial.

Sucking in a breath, he blew it out roughly and said, "It wasn't kids, Piper. It was someone looking for something they didn't find."

Piper shook her head, so violently it sent the long strands of her hair shifting against her shoulders. "What could I possibly have that's so important?"

He hesitated because bringing it up might rouse painful memories for her, but he had no choice. "Is there anything your husband might have had, that he might have given you—"

"Nothing," she shot back quickly. "He hadn't been home for months because he was on deployment and then he was killed. They sent me his things…"

A soft hitch of her breath warned him she was about to cry. He reached out and took her hand into his, offering comfort.

He said nothing else, the silence in the cab of his pickup broken by Piper's soft, hiccuping cries and sniffles.

In front of her home, he parked the pickup and swiveled to face her. "Are you okay?"

She swiped at her tears with one hand since she still gripped his hand tightly. "I'm okay. Thank you for everything."

He nodded. "Let's get you settled for the night."

PIPER SNIFFLED AND released his hand, needing to escape his proximity.

Her brain and heart were in too much turmoil to handle him tonight. "No need, Shane. I'm okay."

A harsh laugh escaped him. "There's no way I'm letting you go in alone."

She could continue to argue with him, but it was just wasting her breath. "Okay. Let's go."

Rushing from his pickup, she walked up her driveway to the path leading to her front door, Shane hot on her heels. She unlocked the door and as soon as she entered, the unfamiliar beep-beep-beep of the alarm pad warned her she only had 120 seconds before the siren would go off. At the sound of the beeping, Decoy and Chipper came running out to jump all over her legs.

"Sit," she commanded, and Shane had to repeat the command before the dogs complied.

Hands shaking, she fumbled at first, but then punched in the code Shane and she had set.

The beeping ended and Piper kneeled to rub the dogs' heads. She scooped up Chipper and the puppy licked her face, making her smile.

But that smile faded as she met Shane's gaze. It was intense and way too focused on her. "I'll be fine. You don't need to worry."

He nodded. "Just to make sure, I'll leave Decoy with you. He didn't do all that well with those attack commands, but he's still big enough to scare someone off."

Piper hoped she wouldn't need to use any attack commands, but just in case…

"Thank you. I'll take good care of him," she said and rubbed Decoy's ears. The dog sidled up to her, happy for the attention. "Good boy."

"I know you will, but… Take good care of yourself as well. I'll see you in the morning," he said and took a step back into the alcove by her front door. He gestured to the alarm pad and said, "Lock up and set that thing."

"I will," she said, but delayed, hand on the edge of the door. Saying "thanks" seemed like so little considering all that he'd done for her in the last few days. But anything else would only complicate things even more.

"Thanks," she said, but quickly added, "We can start training again in the morning."

Her words lightened his features and a quick smile skipped across his lips. "I'd like that."

"I would, too," she said and quickly closed the door.

## Chapter Thirteen

*I'll settle for that*, Shane thought as he ambled across her front lawn to his RV.

*She has the alarm and Chipper and Decoy and me*, he reminded himself. Just in case, he'd have the shotgun he used to protect against predators loaded and ready for use. But first, he did a cautious walk around her property, searching for signs that anyone was nearby again and checking to see that all the doors and windows were secured. Satisfied, he headed for his RV.

Inside the RV, he stripped down to his skivvies, but then slipped into sweats and a T-shirt and placed his boots by the front door in case he had to go running to protect Piper.

Normally he'd have a finger of scotch to relax, but not tonight. He needed to be alert and he had something to do before he went to sleep.

He swiped his phone open and dialed a friend who was stationed at Fort Irwin. A friend with lots of contacts on the base and over at Camp Pendleton. Piper had offhandedly mentioned during their sessions that her husband had trained and deployed from there.

"As I live and breathe, how are you, Shane?" his friend said.

"Living the dream, Walt," he said, repeating the joke they'd always shared when they'd been hunkering down in Afghanistan together on a mission. Like him, Walt had taken a training position, but he'd chosen to be stationed at Fort Irwin.

"But seriously, I'm doing well. How about you?" he said.

"Good. Wife and I have been talking about me finally putting in my papers," Walt said.

"It'll be a big change," Shane said, thinking about how many things he'd had to deal with the last few months since he'd retired.

"Yeah, I get it, man. It's a scary thought, but hell. We've faced scarier, haven't we?"

They had, time and time again. Walt had always watched his six and that's why he knew that Walt would help with what he was about to ask.

"I need a favor."

"Just ask, Shane," Walt said, but Shane hesitated, unsure if it would become a Pandora's box that once opened couldn't be sealed.

"Shane?" Walt pressed at his reticence.

Shane pushed on. "I have a friend who's been having some trouble. Her husband was a Marine who was killed in Iraq about four years ago. I think the trouble may have to do with his last deployment."

"What's his name?"

"David Lambert. He was with the Twenty-Sixth Marine Expeditionary Unit," Shane advised.

"If I remember correctly, they were sent into the

Mosul area to help battle ISIS," Walt said and, in the background, he heard Walt's wife calling out to him. "Honey, are you coming to bed?"

"Be there in a second," his friend responded before coming back on the line. "I can't guarantee anything, but I'll see what I can find out."

"Thanks, Walt. I'd really appreciate that."

They ended the call and Shane got ready for bed.

It was a cool night, so he opened the windows in his bedroom to let in the night air as well as any sounds that shouldn't be there, like the rumble of a pickup's engine.

But it was quiet except for the hoot of an owl in the distance and the rustle of the breeze that brought with it the scent of pine and fir. A warbling trio of notes drifted in on the breeze. It was repeated a few seconds later with another trio of tones, slightly different from the first.

He smiled. A mockingbird showing off his singing skills.

He lay down in bed and closed his eyes, the night sounds enveloping him in their peace. Bringing him solace as he drifted off.

But soon his peace was shattered once again by the nightmare.

The blast of the explosion and the ringing of his ears that brought with it an unnatural silence.

His throat dry thanks to the dust and debris filling the air. Choking him as he struggled to breathe.

The weight of the concrete, wood and glass that had once been the building pressed on his chest and legs, trapping him.

He reached out, searching for the familiar touch of

Decoy's wet nose and his smooth fur. The slight huff of his breath against the palm of Shane's hand, but it wasn't there.

He shot up in bed, breathing heavily. The cool breeze chilled his sweat-dampened skin, rousing goose bumps.

Wrapping his arms around himself, he slipped from bed and went into the living room area, where he grabbed a blanket, lay down on the couch and flipped on the television.

He found a channel with a program where the narrator had that flat, droning voice that soon became mind-numbing. Just what he needed.

But even that tedious narrative wasn't enough to keep other thoughts at bay.

Thoughts about Piper and who might have broken into her home. Whether they were done with Piper or if she was in continued danger.

When the first rays of light pierced the edges of the shades, Shane was still awake. He was still worried about what was happening with Piper, but for today, it was time to try and get back to normal.

SHANE WAS LEANING against the fender of his pickup, waiting for her, when she walked out of the house, Decoy and Chipper dogging her heels, happy to be outside.

At the sight of him, her heart skipped a beat.

He was so handsome. His jeans hugged a flat midsection and long lean legs. The hoodie he wore against the slight morning chill stretched tight across his shoulders.

His blue eyes were as bright as the morning sky, but there were shadows beneath, as if he hadn't slept well.

She walked up to him and laid a hand on his chest, sensing he needed soothing. The muscles beneath her hand were hard, his heartbeat strong and steady. "You look a little beat."

His shoulders went up and down in a careless gesture and he covered her hand with his. Rubbed it gently. "I'm okay. A little tired. How about you?"

Surprisingly, she'd slept better than expected. "I'm good. I slept well thanks to these guys."

She bent to rub the heads and ears of both dogs, who ate up her attention, but when she looked up, her gaze locked with his and she realized he needed her care just as much, maybe more.

She straightened and cupped his jaw. Ran her thumb across his lips, the gesture meant to comfort, but it did anything but.

Her heart pounded in her chest at the heat in his blue-eyed gaze and the way he laid a hand at her waist and drew her close. She took a step closer to him and rose on tiptoes, but the sudden sound of a car pulling up jerked them apart.

A police cruiser had stopped in front of her home, but it wasn't Ava and Brady who stepped out. Lieutenant Margaret Avery, one of the most senior officers in the Jasper PD, exited the car with rookie Officer Jason Wright. Tashya's Jason.

"Good morning," Margaret said as Jason and she approached them. Her keen gaze assessed the situation between her and Shane, bringing a smile to the police officer's face, but hot color to Piper's cheeks.

"Good morning. This is Lieutenant Avery," Piper said, introducing her to Shane.

Shane shook the older woman's hand. "Nice to meet you."

"I wish it was under different circumstances, Shane. We have good news, however. Would you like to provide a report, Officer Wright?"

Clearly this was intended to help Jason learn some of the ropes and if he was working with Margaret, he was lucky. A longtime veteran of Jasper PD, she'd earned her colleagues' respect with her wonderful investigative work and her compassion when dealing with sensitive circumstances. Normally that would mean domestic violence or special victims, but she suspected Chief Walters may have decided to treat her case as one of those sensitive circumstances, explaining the unusual visit from the officers.

"Yes, Lieutenant. We were able to get a useable partial print from one of the doors and are processing it against the various databases for a match. We likewise have solid casts of shoe prints and tire tracks and are working on identifying them. We also have DNA samples from some cigarette butts that are being processed."

"Thank you, Officer Wright," she said, having to bite back her more familiar use of his given name.

"We will find out who is behind this, Piper. And we'll be keeping up our patrols in case he comes back," Margaret said, the blue gaze beneath her bangs of brown hair filled with kindness.

But the thought that her intruder might come back sent a chill through her and she wavered, leaning back into Shane, who offered her support.

Margaret reached out and laid a hand on Piper's arm.

"We will get him. And I understand you've taken precautions."

Shane was the one to respond since she was still too shaken by the thought of the intruder's return.

"WE HAVE. WE'VE INSTALLED a security system and I'll be staying here until we know Piper is safe," Shane said, but omitted any mention of his own investigations into the identity of the burglar and the reasons for the mayhem he'd inflicted on Piper and her home.

The lieutenant nodded. She was a handsome woman with chin-length brown hair and intelligent blue eyes, and she was in excellent physical shape. She looked like she could take care of herself and others, which reassured him.

"Thank you for watching out for Piper. We really appreciate what she and Emma do for Jasper PD," the lieutenant said and gazed at Piper with real affection.

"Let's get going, Officer Wright. We need to check the local pawn shops for Piper's rings," Margaret said.

Jason smiled at the lieutenant, not fazed by her order, which hinted at how much respect he had for his superior.

He faced them, touched the brim of his baseball cap and said, "See you later."

"See you, Jason," Piper said and once the two officers were gone, she faced him, her features filled with worry.

"Even if he comes back, we're ready for him, Piper. Don't worry," he said, even though he knew the words would do little to appease her. But what would help was to get her back to work and her normal routine.

"I'm ready to get back to training if you are."

She nodded and gazed at the two dogs who were peacefully snuggled together at their feet. "I'm ready. We have only a little more than a week before you go."

He winced as she said it, well aware of the looming deadline for his departure.

Her words prompted them into action and a tense silence as they loaded the dogs into his pickup and did the short drive to the DCA grounds.

The silence persisted as they walked into the training ring and resumed their exercises with Decoy, having him run through the various verbal and hand signals as well as the agility course.

Shane was happy to see him go through the paces without hesitation, even when Chipper tried to chase after him, wanting to be like her pal.

"Chipper, sit," Piper commanded but had to repeat it several times before the little dog complied. Her frustration was obvious and unusual for her since she was typically more patient.

"It's okay, Piper," he said when he thought he detected the glimmer of tears in her eyes.

She sniffled. "I'm okay, Shane. I just want you to be as prepared as you can be when you go."

And there it was again, but in a way he understood. She was preparing herself for his departure by reminding herself that he would go. Reminding him that their time together was limited.

He didn't want her to think she was failing him. Laying a hand on her shoulder, he gave her a reassuring squeeze and said, "You're doing a great job. We've learned so much."

She nodded and looked away, avoiding his gaze. "But there's so much more to learn. Maybe we can start some scent training. I'll go prepare it," she said and didn't wait for his reply.

PIPER RUSHED OFF, needing distance from Shane and the reminder that he and Decoy would soon be gone.

She was determined that when they left, they'd be totally ready to continue their search and rescue training with another group.

In the DCA offices, she went straight to the equipment locker and prepped the materials they'd need to start the scent work with Decoy.

She carefully wetted some cotton swabs with birch oil, using gloves and tweezers so that the scent would only be on the object Decoy would have to find and not her.

When she returned to the ring, Shane was playing with the two dogs, laughing and smiling as they circled him or jumped up onto his legs. She'd heard his occasional laughter in the last weeks, but nothing like this unrestrained carefree happiness.

It chased away some of the worry that had plagued her ever since someone had trashed her home and stolen her wedding rings. Besides the few belongings she'd kept from David, mostly his military items, they were the only reminders of the husband she'd loved and lost way too soon.

Well, the only reminders besides her memories of David. Happy memories mixed together with the sadness and worry she'd feel whenever he left for a deployment.

Leaving being something that Shane would do as well.

Pain filled her heart, but she sucked in a breath and pushed it away, intending to enjoy whatever moments she had left with Shane.

She walked over to the trio and Shane pushed off his haunches, still laughing and smiling. He was even handsomer when he smiled, and it took years off his features.

"Are you ready?"

At his nod, she handed him a small tin with several holes punched in the top. "Hold this in one hand and a treat in the other. Let Decoy eat the treat and after, bring another treat to the tin and let him smell it. Reinforce that by giving him the treat and then switch hands."

He did as she instructed and Decoy, good boy that he was, immediately caught on. They repeated the exercise over and over, and Decoy obeyed. They challenged him by hiding the tin behind one of the fence posts and after giving Decoy the "search" command, he sniffed all around the ring. It took a few minutes, but Decoy finally paused by the fence post, sat and started barking, just like he'd been trained.

"Good boy," Piper said, then gave him a treat and rubbed his ears and head.

"He is a good boy," Shane said, standing beside them.

"A champ," Piper said and laughed as Chipper sat next to Decoy and barked as well, copying her friend's actions.

"You, too, Chipper," Piper said and bent to reward the dog with a treat and affection.

"Are you game to try this on the trail?" she asked.

Shane nodded and said, "I'm game."

SHANE WAS PLEASED with how the afternoon training had gone. Decoy had not only been able to find the little tin box Piper had prepared, but also a pair of her work gloves and a doughnut, courtesy of Barbara, who decided the doughnut's sacrifice would help her watch her waist.

When they returned to Piper's home, there were no signs that anyone had been there, but he checked all around the grounds to make sure. Satisfied, they'd split up to shower and get ready to go to dinner together.

Shane had no intention of leaving Piper alone just in case her intruder decided to come back.

He was just getting out of the shower when his phone rang. He ambled over to it and picked up when he realized it was Walt calling.

"Good afternoon, Walt. Please tell me you found something," he said and wiped a towel across his hair to dry it.

"Something, but I'm still working on it," Walt said.

"What have you got?" Shane asked, impatient to hear what his friend would say.

"I reached out to some of my Marine buddies who were familiar with Lambert's unit. Rumor had it that some of the men found a cache of relics that were believed to have been destroyed when ISIS occupied the Mosul Museum. The relics the Marines found were reported to their superiors and were supposed to have been safeguarded and returned to the Iraqis, but somehow they disappeared again."

Shane didn't like where this was going but had to press forward to keep Piper safe. "Do you know who these men were?"

"Lambert and some others. I'm still working on finding out more. My contact was going to ask around and possibly get me some paperwork with additional information."

Shane juggled the phone while trying to wrap the towel around his waist as a knock came at his door. "I have to go, but thanks for everything. I really appreciate it."

"Not a problem, Shane. You saved my butt more than once. It's the least I can do," Walt said and hung up.

Shane dropped the phone on his kitchen counter, grabbed the towel with one hand and opened the door.

Piper stood there, dressed and ready to go.

Bright red erupted up her neck and across the creamy skin of her face as she took in his nakedness.

"Um, um, I came over to see if you were ready," she said and gestured to his chest before mumbling a curse and shaking her head.

"I won't be long. Do you want to come in?" he said although he wasn't sure her being with him half-naked in such close quarters was the best idea. Mostly because he wanted her to put her hands on him.

Her hesitation spoke volumes about where her brain was going as well, but something made him ask again.

"So? Do you want to come in?" he said and hoped she wouldn't refuse.

# Chapter Fourteen

*Come in?* she thought. It was like the proverbial spider inviting in the fly, but it would seem rude to refuse.

"S-s-ure," she said, but tried to avoid the sight of his naked chest and legs. Not that she would forget the way he looked, all lean hard muscle. The scar on one shoulder and another farther down on his ribs. What looked like a burn angling down one hip and beneath the edge of the towel.

*Look away, Piper. Don't touch*, she told herself as she stepped into the spacious RV.

Inside, he pointed to the couch in a living room area and said, "I'll only be a minute."

He turned to walk to his bedroom, displaying the perfect line of his back and the marred skin on his right shoulder: the injury that had forced him to leave the Army and had brought him to her.

When the door closed behind him, she breathed a sigh of relief. It was hard enough being around Shane while they were training. Having him close the last few days had been difficult because she was growing more and more used to having him around.

That would only bring heartbreak.

She reminded herself of that as she waited, and it
didn't take long for Shane to come out, dressed in jeans
that hugged his powerful legs and a white cotton shirt
with dark mother-of-pearl buttons. He'd gotten some
color in the two weeks they'd been working together,
and the tan popped against the white of his shirt. But
the tan couldn't hide the dark circles beneath his eyes,
a testament to the fact he might not be sleeping well.

"I'm ready," he said.

"Good," she said and rushed to his door, eager to escape the confines of the RV, which seemed suddenly
too small with his powerful presence.

She stepped onto her lawn and didn't wait for him
to walk across to her Jeep. At his questioning glance,
she said, "I feel like driving today. Is that a problem?"

He grinned and said, "Not at all."

She hopped up into the driver's seat and Shane joined
her. "I'm a little tired of burgers and beer. There's a
nice Italian place not far from the brewery and diner."

"That sounds good. I haven't had a decent plate of
pasta in a while," he said and rubbed his stomach.

"Great," she said and pulled out of her driveway.

There wasn't much traffic, and Shane seemed to notice. "Not many people around today."

With a shrug, she said, "It'll start getting busier in
May when the hikers and fishermen visit. People also
come looking for the handmade furniture that's made
in the area. But the busiest time is in July when we have
the annual Salmon River Festival."

"Sounds like a lot of fun," he said.

She shot a quick look in his direction and realized he
was watching her intently. Her heartbeat raced a little

at his perusal. She tore her gaze back to the road and said, "It is. You should think about coming back for it."

She nearly bit her lip at how it sounded, but Shane, gentleman that he was, said, "Thanks. I will think about it."

With little traffic, they were soon cruising down Main Street and past the diner and the alley leading to the brewery. Luck was on their side as there was an open spot just a few doors down from the restaurant. But inside the restaurant the tables were all full and they had to wait for about ten minutes before one opened up.

Once they were seated, the waitress came over to hand them menus and take their drink orders. She ordered a glass of Chianti, but Shane just got some pop. At her questioning look, he said, "Need to stay sharp."

Sharp because he expected more trouble, which dimmed her generally good mood.

She set aside her menu, knowing she would order her favorite. Shane did the same just seconds later and said, "What are you getting?"

"Eggplant parmigiana with a big mound of angel hair pasta is my go-to," she said and gestured with her hands to demonstrate just how big a mound of pasta she hoped to eat.

He chuckled and mimicked her. "That big, huh?"

She did the action again. "That big."

A lopsided smile slipped across his lips, but the waitress came over that moment to set down their drinks and take their orders.

Piper placed her order, followed by Shane, but when he did, he teased her by showing the waitress just how big a pile of pasta he wanted.

"A big man like you must get mighty hungry," the waitress said, and eyed Shane in a way that Piper didn't much like. She also lingered way too long after getting his order.

"Thanks, Brandy" she said, making it clear to Brandy that it was time to go.

SHANE KNEW IT was wrong of him, but he couldn't resist. "Jealous?"

Piper laughed, trying to hide her embarrassment, but the flush on her face gave it all away. "She's way too old for you, Shane."

Brandy was probably close to fifty and definitely not his type. He preferred intelligent, determined, barely-over-thirty dog trainers with intense green eyes and long red hair he could imagine wrapped around him as they made love.

And at that moment, he was most grateful for the table that hid his reaction to that thought. Judging from the way Piper's gaze darkened to the color of shadows in a forest at night, it was obvious she might have guessed where his brain had gone and that her brain had traveled to a similar place.

He coughed to fight his reaction and reached for a piece of bread from the basket in the middle of the table. She reached for it at the same time and their hands grazed over the slices of Italian bread.

He fought the reaction to jerk his hand back and instead steadily gestured to the basket. "Please, go ahead."

She hastily grabbed a slice and slowly began buttering it.

He did the same, taking his time because he was sure

it wasn't the right time to ask about her husband. Let her get her fill of that mound of pasta and some of the red wine. Let her relax for a little bit because the last couple of days had been awful.

Because of that, he tried to keep it light. "Decoy did an amazing job today, didn't he?"

"He did. He truly was born to be a search and rescue dog. You're going to be wonderful together," she said and sipped her wine, but her hand trembled as she did so, reminding him that even this topic was a minefield.

"Again, thanks to you and the DCA, It's a wonderful thing you and Emma do," he said, steering the conversation away from where the future might take them.

"Thank you, but it's just as rewarding for us when clients do well with the training," Piper said.

"I can imagine. I used to feel the same way when I had a soldier who excelled at sharpshooting," Shane said.

Piper hesitated, but then blurted out, "Do you miss it?"

With a shrug, Shane said, "I did, but I'm finding this new life…interesting."

Piper arched a brow. "Interesting?"

The waitress came by at that moment with their meals, placing the plates before them, and sparing him from having to explain his comment.

As Piper had indicated, the portions of pasta were generous, and the earthy scent of garlic and sweet tomatoes wafted up to him from his plate of chicken parmigiana. His stomach rumbled noisily thanks to the aromas.

"Looks great," he said and dug in, as did Piper, but he urged her to continue.

"You met Emma in college?" he asked, changing the topic of their earlier conversation.

Piper sliced off a piece of her eggplant and paused with it halfway to her mouth. "We did. We hit it off right away. Roomed together and kept in touch once we graduated."

Since he knew the rest of the story would involve how she married her husband and his death, he kept silent so they could satisfy their hunger and eat in peace.

Despite the size of the portion, he managed to eat all of it because he had underestimated his appetite. But Piper still had a good amount of pasta left and as the waitress walked by, she asked for a container.

"It's always more than I can eat, and I like to make spaghetti pie with the leftovers," she explained at his curious look.

"My mom used to make that for me." She had made the most of whatever they had because money had been tight in their family.

"Where do your mom and dad live?" she asked.

With a tight smile, he said, "They're both gone. Died in a car accident right after I graduated high school. It's one of the reasons I decided to enlist. Well, that and 9/11. I needed to get away."

PIPER TOTALLY UNDERSTOOD. After David's death she'd been floundering and coming to Emma's had been her salvation in more ways than one. It had not only let her get away from the daily reminders of her loss, but it had also given her a whole new career and life.

Sensing his upset, she laid a hand on his and stroked his skin with her thumb. "I'm sorry. I know how hard it is when you lose people you love."

The muscles of his hand tightened before he turned it over and took hold of hers. "I know you know. Losing your husband... What was he like?"

She dug past the pain, remembering David's easy smile and grace. How he could ride a wave as if he and the surfboard were one. Spending lazy Sunday mornings in bed, reading the funnies and drinking coffee before they would go for a jog together.

Her throat choked up with the threat of incipient tears as she said, "He was a good man. Caring. Honorable."

A tight smile came to Shane's lips with that last word. Focusing on his features, she said, "Is there something that you're not telling me?"

Shane did a quick look around the room, and she tracked his gaze. Chief Walters and Theresa were at a table not all that far away. In a distant corner, Lieutenant Avery sat with another police officer she didn't recognize. If it got heated with Shane, she didn't want it to be in front of people she knew.

"Maybe we should discuss this in private," she said and signaled the waitress to bring the check.

But when Brandy did, Shane snagged it. "My treat. The food was great."

She didn't argue with him, deciding to save herself for what she suspected would be a more important battle. "Thank you."

He slipped several bills into the wallet, rose and held out his hand to her, but she ignored it and hurried from the restaurant.

She restarted the conversation as soon as she was be-hind the wheel and had begun the drive home. "What is it you're not telling me?"

Shane rubbed a hand across his mouth and then down his jaw. "I think it should wait until we get home."

She wanted to scream that it wasn't their home, it was her home and she'd only let him park on her lawn because he was helping her. The reminder that he was helping her dimmed her anger, but only a little.

They hurried home in silence. She jerked the Jeep to a halt in her driveway and stormed into her house, Shane hot on her heels. She slammed the door shut with a resounding thud and Decoy and Chipper came run-ning. But as if sensing that something wasn't right, they immediately rushed back toward Chipper's crate near the sliding doors in the kitchen area.

"I was only trying to help, Piper. You have to believe that," Shane said, hands held out in pleading.

"What did you do?" she said, arms crossed in front of her.

Shane dragged a hand through the longer strands of hair at the top of his head and blew out a harsh breath. Shaking his head, he said, "I reached out to a friend who might have connections at Camp Pendleton."

She wagged her head so furiously strands of hair flew across her face. She yanked them back and stalked into the center of her living room. Pacing back and forth for a second, she whirled and faced Shane. "You were checking into David? His service?"

Shane took a faltering step forward. "You heard Ava the other day. Someone was looking for something spe-cific."

"What could I possibly have and what does it have to do with David?" she argued, not wanting to believe that the theft could have anything to do with her dead husband.

Shane motioned to the sofa. "I think you should sit down."

## Chapter Fifteen

The last thing Shane wanted to do was hurt Piper or dirty the memory of her late husband. But it was possible that whatever had happened in Iraq was responsible for what was happening now in Jasper. Much like it was also possible that her husband had had nothing to do with any of it. Because of that, he chose his words carefully.

"When ISIS took over Mosul, they destroyed many relics in the Mosul Museum and after that, the museum was ransacked. Many precious artifacts were taken."

Piper peered at him, clearly confused. "What does this have to do with David?"

"My contact says that there are rumors that a group of Marines on a mission found some of the missing relics. They were supposed to keep the relics safe until they were returned to the Iraqis."

Her eyes widened as his words sank in. "You think David was one of the Marines?"

Nodding, he reached out to lay a hand on hers, but she shied away. "My friend said that it was David and his squad, but he's trying to find out more."

Piper shook her head. "David would never steal anything. Never."

"I believe you, but it's possible someone else thinks that he did. Maybe that's why they trashed your house and went through your husband's belongings," Shane said, trying to convince her, not that he could.

"If David had these relics, they would have been with his things. Those are the only things that came from Iraq. I'll go get them," she said and shot to her feet.

SHANE UNDERSTOOD HOW difficult this was for Piper. He was basically accusing the man she had loved of being a thief.

He hoped that their examination of his things would not reveal any of the relics. But if they didn't, he wasn't sure that meant Piper was safe because whoever had broken in believed that she had something of value.

When Piper returned with the duffel, he helped her place it on the sofa between them. With care she removed one item after another and laid them on the coffee table. Once the bag was empty, he examined it for any kind of hidden compartment, but there was none.

"Nothing here," he said, but Piper didn't say a thing. She only handed him David's dress uniform jacket. His medals and campaign ribbons were still on the breast of the jacket. Cautiously he examined all the seams, the lining and the pockets. Again, nothing.

Gently he folded the uniform and returned it to the duffel.

He did the same with each of the other garments, cautiously inspecting each item before respectfully returning it to the bag.

When he was done, it was clear that there was nothing hidden in any of Lambert's things.

He met Piper's gaze and it was chilly, like evergreens glazed over from a winter ice storm.

"I'm sorry we had to do this," he said and zipped the duffel closed. He grabbed hold of it and stood. "Let me put this back for you."

"I'll do it," she said and snatched the bag from him.

She marched from the room, and he heard her rummaging about in her bedroom, probably as she returned the duffel to where she kept it. But she didn't come back right away, prompting worry.

He lumbered to her door, feeling guilty that he'd put her through something that had brought her pain.

She sat on her bed, tears streaming down her face, and his heart hurt for her.

He walked over, sat beside her and took her into his arms. She was stiff at first, but eventually relaxed against him and wrapped her arms around him.

"I'm sorry, Piper. I didn't mean to cause you any pain."

She nodded and sniffled. "I know you were only trying to help, but you have to believe me that David would never do something like that."

He tucked her head beneath his chin and stroked her back, soothing her. "I do believe you, Piper. But the problem is that someone else may think your husband has these things."

Piper did an unsteady bop of her head and shifted away from him. "And they won't stop until they find it."

While he didn't want to agree with her, she was right.

"They won't. But we're ready for them now. The house is secured, and you've got Chipper and Decoy with you. I'll be right outside."

She offered him a weak smile and wiped away the trails of her tears. Gazing up at him, she said, "I'm sorry I was curt with you."

He stroked her back with his hand and said, "I understand. If you had accused one of my loved ones, I'd have been upset as well."

Nodding, she said, "I guess we keep on searching for why someone is doing this."

"We do. Hopefully my friend will have more for us shortly."

He cupped her cheek and ran his thumb across her tear-dampened skin. Met her gaze, dark with emotion now. She worried her lower lip with her teeth as desire slowly replaced her upset. He lowered his head until her warm breath spilled against his lips, but then reminded himself of who she was, who he was and why this shouldn't happen.

He bolted to his feet, nearly upending her as she sat on the edge of the bed. She teetered as she rose, laying a hand on his arm for stability, and he slipped his arm through hers, offering support.

Together they tottered to the front door, Shane buoying an unsteady Piper.

At the door, he faced her, and they stood there for long moments, uncertain. But then he bent quickly and brushed a quick kiss on her lips.

"See you in the morning. Lock up," he said and rushed out the door.

PIPER CLOSED THE DOOR, locked it and then leaned against it. She brushed fingers across her lips, remembering his brief kiss. Dazed by it and the fact she wished it had been more.

Shaking her head, she pushed off the door and used the keypad to set the alarm. But she realized the dogs hadn't gone out that night yet and so she disarmed the system, walked over to Decoy and Chipper and slipped on their leashes. She opened the sliding door and took them outside, rambling around the edges of her yard while the dogs relieved themselves. She hurried back into the house and secured the doors, including slipping in the piece of wood that Shane had cut to place in the sliding door rail so it couldn't be easily opened even if the lock was picked.

Resetting the alarm, she took the dogs with her into her bedroom, and they snuggled together on the dog bed at one side of the room.

Even though it was late, and she was weary from the weight of the emotions roused that night, sleep eluded her.

She didn't have a television in her bedroom, so she went back into the living room, Chipper and Decoy trailing after her. As she did so, she walked by the sliding doors and noticed the play of shadows and light from the back of Shane's RV. His bedroom if she remembered correctly from her brief visit earlier that night.

He wasn't able to sleep either.

She hunkered down on the couch and flipped on the television. Decoy spread out on the floor by her feet while Chipper clambered up at the end of the sofa.

Their presence was calming and after a few minutes, her eyes slowly drifted closed, but then something jolted her awake again.

Had it been a shout? she wondered and listened carefully, but there was only the quiet of the night.

THE WINDOWS AT the front of the house provided a clear view into the living room.

He watched through his binoculars as Lambert's widow entered the room, the two dogs following behind her.

He lost sight of her as she settled onto the couch and soon the flashes of light and dark told him she'd turned on the television, clearly settling in for the night.

He mumbled a curse. He'd been hoping that she'd stay away at her friend's ranch, but now she was already back, and the place had been secured as if it was Fort Knox. It would be difficult to get back inside the house without setting off alarms.

He'd only just emptied Lambert's duffel bag when he'd seen them coming through the meadow and had to escape, nearly running them over in the process. At least he'd grabbed her rings to make it look like a robbery and maybe provide him some money if he could find somewhere to pawn the rings without alerting the cops.

He had to be able to get back in there and look for the relics. He was sure Lambert had sent them to his wife before he'd been killed on one of their missions. The only other person who'd had access to them had been Buck, but he'd visited his friend who had denied having the treasures. Plus, Buck wasn't living the high life, relying on his family's business to give him a clerk's job that barely paid his expenses.

He hadn't been as lucky. No one wanted to hire someone who had been dishonorably discharged, forcing him to steal to live.

But what he'd taken so far was peanuts compared with what Lambert's widow had in her possession. If he could grab the relics from her, he could sell them for millions on the black market.

Setting down the binoculars, he climbed back into the blue pickup he'd stolen in Boise. He'd have to ditch it and find another ride because he was sure the police would be looking out for it. Tonight, he'd spend the night in the abandoned cabin he'd broken into to hide when he realized he'd have to stalk Piper longer than he'd originally thought.

In the morning he'd hightail it to McCall and pick up a different a ride and then come back to Jasper and be patient. When the time was right, he'd grab Piper and get her to tell him where she had the relics her husband had sent her.

Once she revealed where the treasures were, everything would be okay in his world.

He just had to wait and watch.

## Chapter Sixteen

The nightmare had raked its claws into him again last night.

He woke groggily, the weight of it dragging on him emotionally, drained physically by the lack of sleep.

But it wasn't the first time he'd gone without rest. He had sometimes spent days without sleeping while on a mission, pushing on because he had to for the sake of the assignment and his fellow soldiers.

Now he had to do it for Piper's sake.

He forced himself from bed and fixed a big cup of coffee. Stood in his kitchen watching as Piper slipped out the sliding doors and walked the two dogs.

She was fully dressed, warning him that he should be getting ready for their daily training session. Not to mention avoid another embarrassing incident like what had happened the night before when she had caught him half-naked.

He slugged back a mouthful of coffee, wincing as the heat of it burned down his throat.

Rushing into his bedroom, he dressed for the day, slipping on a T-shirt and layering a flannel shirt over it. There was still the chill of winter in the early morning, but that quickly gave way to heat as the sun rose.

He had just finished putting on his work boots and making himself a to-go cup of coffee when a light knock came at his door.

Opening it, he wasn't surprised to see Piper at the door with the two dogs.

"Good morning, Piper," he said and stepped out onto the grass of her side lawn.

"Is it a good morning?" she said, eyeing him with concern. "You look tired."

"A little tired. I didn't sleep well," he admitted, but didn't say more, unwilling to share the reason for why it had been a rough night.

He somehow made it through the day's training and dinner with Emma, who opened her home to them. It was a pleasant dinner with no talk about the break-in, just the training. Her vet tech, Tashya, and her boyfriend, Officer Jason Wright, had come in just as they were having dessert and coffee and joined them. Luckily, Tashya and Jason had likewise avoided talk about Piper's intruder, especially since Shane turned the discussion to them.

"Have you two been dating long?" he asked, and the two twenty-somethings shared a loving look.

"About four years, but we've known each other for longer. Emma fostered both Tashya and me and that's how we met," Jason said, and Emma explained.

"Since I was lucky enough to be fostered and then adopted by the Danielses, I decided to honor them by also fostering young people who needed help," she said.

"I was fourteen when Emma took me in and changed

my life. It's thanks to her I was able to finish vet tech school," Tashya added and peered at Emma with adoration.

"Gonzo told me you're helping at-risk kids now as well," he said, wanting to know more about what else happened at the DCA besides the dog training.

Emma nodded and gestured to Piper. "We do. We have them do chores around the property and work with the dogs. It helps them learn responsibility and, like Jason, a few of them have gone on to become police officers. As for the others, most have stayed out of trouble."

But not all, he heard in her words. Although he didn't ask it, he wondered again if one of those kids who hadn't been saved was responsible for what was happening at Piper's home.

"It's an amazing thing you've done for so many of us," Jason said and shot Emma a look filled with respect and caring.

"I had to pay it forward," Emma said, obviously grateful for the people who had saved her when she needed it.

He recognized that need to help others. It was one of the reasons he'd chosen to serve in the military.

The rest of the night passed quickly, and he was soon driving Piper back home.

He said good-night to her at the front door, leaving Decoy with her even though the dog helped him chase away the worst of the nightmares. Once he was settled in bed, he flipped on the television and tried to get some sleep, but he was just drifting off when the first tendrils of the nightmare crept into his brain.

The dust and debris. Searing pain in his shoulder. This time, the sounds filled his ears. The moans of someone nearby, trapped like he was. Banging on a pipe, a call for rescue. The rumble of heavy equipment, an excavator waiting to claw through the debris.

He jerked awake, heart pounding heavily. Clammy sweat chilling his body.

Taking several deep breaths, he shoved the dream from his brain and tried to focus on the images on the television. But almost as soon as his eyes closed, the nightmare came again.

It was a pattern that repeated all night long until the first hint of morning light pierced past the edges of his blinds, warning that he had to get out of bed and prepare for the day.

Not even an ice-cold shower could drive away the lethargy.

When he opened the door after Piper's knock, her gaze traveled over his features, but she thankfully didn't say anything. At least not then.

After he'd had trouble putting Decoy through some of the search and rescue exercises, Piper stopped the training session. Hands on her hips, she eyed him up and down and said, "You don't look too good, and you've been really off today."

He rubbed the stubble on his jaw since he hadn't felt steady enough to shave, especially since the lack of sleep was also making his shoulder act up more than normal. He'd had a dull ache in it all day and his hand had been shakier than usual. Maybe because he was sitting in weird positions while he tried to get to sleep.

"I haven't been sleeping well," he admitted because to deny that something wasn't up with him would be impossible.

PIPER STRODE TO him until she was barely a foot away and had to tilt her head back to look at him thanks to his much greater height. She laid a hand on his chest. The cotton of his dark blue T-shirt was smooth beneath her hand. His muscles were tense, his heartbeat a heavy lub-dub beneath her palm. A muscle ticked along his jaw and she recognized the stance well.

Her husband could sometimes be the strong silent type, but David hadn't built up as many walls as Shane. She had seen them on the very first day because she'd constructed some of her own. She had thought that in the last few weeks together, they'd both torn down some of their defenses, but clearly Shane had put up his shields again in the last couple of days.

Wanting to restore the connection they'd started to share, she smoothed her hand across his chest and said, "You can tell me, Shane. I won't judge."

He clenched his jaw and avoided her gaze until she cupped his cheek with her other hand and applied gentle pressure to urge him to face her.

His blue gaze was as tumultuous as the Salmon River when the spring thaw on the mountains sent waters cascading down it. But as she stroked his chest again and shifted her other hand to brush back a lock of the longish hair at the top of his head, he relaxed beneath her caring touch.

"I have nightmares," he said in so low a whisper she

almost didn't hear it. But the pain of it reached deep inside her.

"It's okay if you do. You've seen things none of us can even imagine," she said, recalling her husband's restless nights when he'd be home between deployments.

He nodded and, in a stronger voice, said, "I have. They're usually about being trapped beneath the rubble of the building."

"Is that why you want to do search and rescue?" she asked, surprising herself that she hadn't asked him about his motivation earlier.

With a shake of his head, he said, "No. At first I didn't know what I wanted to do or where to go. The Army had been my whole life, but I didn't want to be a desk jockey."

She glanced at the shoulder that he sometimes rubbed and remembered the scars she'd seen on his body a couple of days earlier. It clicked that his injury had forced his retirement, but before she could say anything, he said, "When Gonzo mentioned it… It made sense since Decoy had rescued me."

She heard what he didn't say. "He saves you at night as well, doesn't he?"

"He does. He helps me get through the nightmares," he said with a nod. "But it's more important that he protects you right now."

Having Decoy with her at night did make her feel better. But for both her and Shane to stay safe, Shane had to be alert as well and he clearly wasn't.

"I think it's time we call it a day and go home. To

my home. You can stay in my spare bedroom," she said, her tone brooking no disagreement.

She pivoted on her heel and marched to his pickup, giving him little time to object. At his vehicle, he did finally protest.

Laying his hand on the door to keep her from opening it, he said, "That's not a good idea, Piper. You can't even begin to imagine what my nightmares are like."

But she could, especially since it occurred to her that the shout she'd heard the other night had been Shane, calling out in the middle of one of his bad dreams.

"You'll have Decoy to help and so will I." It was the least she could do considering all that he'd done to help her in the last couple of weeks.

His jaw tightened again, but he drew in a breath and shakily released it. "Okay. You win."

Trudging away from her to the driver's side, he got in and waited for her to slip into the passenger seat.

When she did, he pulled away and did the short drive back to Piper's home. It was early afternoon because they'd cut short that day's training session, leaving plenty of time for them to pack up some of Shane's things and get him settled in the spare room.

"Why don't you try and take a nap? With everything that's going on I've fallen behind on some paperwork for the DCA and am going to try and catch up with it," she said.

He hesitated, but then nodded and went to the spare room, Decoy and Chipper on his heels, but she called for Chipper to stay with her. To her satisfaction, Chipper complied, and she rewarded the puppy with a body massage and a treat.

After the door to the spare bedroom closed, she sat down at a desk at the far side of the living room and tackled the paperwork. Some were forms intended to confirm Shane and Decoy's training. Others were schedules for future training sessions or prospective clients Emma thought Piper should handle.

They normally discussed prospective clients, which was why Shane's training sessions had been a bit of a surprise. But then again, it had been a last-minute decision on Shane's part from what she could tell, and she hated to admit it, but Emma had been right that she had learned things from working with Shane. Namely, that she was more ready for a relationship than she had thought.

Shane might have had his nightmares the last few days, but she had had dreams of Shane and what it would be like if he wasn't leaving in a little over a week. Dreams of a life she had thought was gone after David's death.

She had never imagined she'd have those dreams again, much less with another military man.

But Shane was no longer in the military, which meant they could have a steady and stable life, unlike the one she'd had with David thanks to his various deployments.

Chipper's whine at her feet snared her attention and reminded her that she'd been sitting for a couple of hours. Which also reminded her that it was almost time for dinner.

A slight drizzle had started after they'd gotten home, bringing a damp chill into the air with the coming of dusk.

They needed something warm to chase away the

chill, so she got out the ingredients to make some chili and corn bread. It was the kind of comfort food her mom used to make and would do well to warm their bellies as well as possibly bring some solace to Shane.

She browned the meat with onions, garlic, some tomato paste and a chipotle pepper with some of the adobo from the can. She added beans and chicken broth and set the pot to simmer. In no time she'd mixed up some corn bread from a mix and had it baking in the oven. Inhaling the earthy scents of the chili and sweetness of the corn bread brought happy memories of her family, who were still living in California. It reminded her that it had been nearly a year since she'd seen them and that it was maybe time to visit.

*Maybe with Shane*, she thought in a moment of hopefulness.

After setting the table, she poured herself a little bit of wine from an open bottle and started prepping the fixings for the chili. She had just finished chopping some scallions when Shane ambled out of the spare bedroom.

He raked his fingers through his hair to smooth down the longer strands that had been sleep tousled. Although there were dark smudges like charcoal beneath his eyes, he seemed a little more alert.

"Feeling better?" she asked, although it was obvious from his posture and the easy smile that flitted across his lips.

"Much. And hungry. That smells delicious."

SHANE WALKED INTO the kitchen area and lifted the cover from the pot with the chili. Inhaling the aromas, he broadened his smile as they brought back wonderful memories. "My mom used to make chili on rainy days," he said and glanced toward the sliding doors where a light sprinkle fell. It was dusk, but there was little light thanks to the clouds obscuring the last of the sun's rays.

As it got a bit darker, the dusk-to-dawn sensor light snapped to life, illuminating a goodly portion of Piper's backyard. He had no doubt that an intruder wouldn't risk entry that way because they'd be too visible.

"I hope the chili will chase the chill away," she said and laughed brightly. "Chili on a chilly day."

He joined in her laughter, grateful for the happier mood. Grateful not to be alone in the RV on such a miserable night.

Covering the chili, he walked to the living room windows and confirmed that the front door light had turned on as well. It shined toward the short alcove before the door and near the garden beneath the living room windows. Realizing that they were totally visible to anyone on the street, he walked over and lowered the window blinds.

Piper noticed his actions but said nothing. She continued cooking and he went over and stood beside her, laying a hand at the small of her back in a gesture that was way too comfortable. Way too normal if they'd been a loving couple.

*Only you aren't*, the little voice in his head challenged. He ignored it, enjoying this easy time with Piper way too much.

"How can I help?" he said.

She gestured to the refrigerator with a tilt of her

head. "There's some sour cream and shredded cheese in the fridge. Hot sauce if you like it. Beer as well."

He walked over, took the items out and laid them on the table she had already set. The place mats were catty-corner to each other, which would bring them close when they ate. He didn't have time to change the setup since she walked over with a plate with some fixings and set it next to what he'd taken out of the fridge.

"Make yourself at home," she said and walked back to the stove, where she ladled chili into deep earthenware bowls. He walked over to take them from her and bring them to the table while she cut squares of corn bread and placed them on another plate.

He waited until she came to the table and sat, then took the spot next to her.

"Enjoy," she said and reached for the fixings to prepare her chili.

"I will," he said and watched as she piled her plate high with the scallions, pimentos, shredded cheddar and hot sauce.

He arched a brow. "No sour cream?"

She grinned and shook her head. "Don't want to drown the chili in too much."

*Like everything she'd piled on the plate already?* he thought with a strangled laugh but kept silent because the smells from the chili and corn bread were way too enticing.

He mimicked what she had done, piling his plate high with fixings. After taking a bite, the heat of the hot sauce and chili had him reaching for the sour cream and the beer to tame the spiciness.

The corn bread also provided the perfect blend of

heat and sweet. He found himself eating bits of corn bread with each forkful of the chili until there was nothing left in his plate and only a little chug of beer in the bottle.

Piper had yet to finish, but when she noticed he was done, she said, "Can I get you more? Another beer?"

He held his hand up to keep her from interrupting her meal. "I can get it. Can I get you anything?"

"There's some butter on the counter if it's not a bother," she said with a smile.

"Not a bother," he replied and loved just how homey the moment felt.

He spooned himself another bowlful but skipped getting a second beer. The nap had helped improve his alertness and he didn't want to dim that with alcohol. Snaring the butter dish from the counter, he returned to the table.

While he ate his second bowl, Piper finished her first, but took another piece of corn bread and slathered it with butter.

He ate a forkful of his chili, swallowed and said, "Did you get your paperwork done?"

She nodded and chewed her corn bread. "I did. I'd fallen a little behind," she said and didn't need to explain why. The last few days had definitely taken time away from her normal schedule.

"Good to hear," he said, and silence filled the air for a few short minutes as they both finished their dinner.

When they were done, they worked together to clear the table, put away the leftover chili and corn bread, and wash dishes, standing beside each other as Shane rinsed and handed dishes to Piper to place them in the dishwasher.

They had just finished cleaning when Shane's phone rang, shattering the companionable chatter they'd been sharing.

Shane whipped the phone from his back pocket, saw that it was Walt and tensed.

As Piper witnessed his reaction, she realized who might be calling.

She gestured to her living room sofa and mouthed, "I'll leave you alone."

Worried the distance to the couch wasn't enough for privacy, he walked down the hall and to the spare bedroom.

"Evening, Walt. How are you?"

"I'm good. How about you? The woman?" Walt asked.

Shane didn't want to delay it any further. "Waiting for news from the police and hopefully you."

Walt laughed and Shane could picture his friend shaking his head to chastise him. "Always direct, but I have some good news for you. It doesn't seem like Lambert had anything to do with the theft of the relics. He reported their discovery so the authorities could recover them before he was killed in action."

"But they weren't recovered," Shane said, wanting to be sure about what Walt was saying.

"They weren't, but like I said, it seems like Lambert is in the clear there. He followed protocol, but two members of his squad apparently didn't. They went AWOL immediately after Lambert was killed and before the authorities could reach the relics."

Shane considered what Walt had said. "The Marines think that those two soldiers stole the treasures?"

"They do, but they had nothing to prove it and certainly not the relics, which are still missing. But they were AWOL and the Marines used that to dishonorably discharge them. I've got those papers for you, but they're heavily redacted," Walt said, and Shane could hear his friend tapping on keys, likely sending him the materials.

"Thank you for this, Walt. It's been a big help," he said and a second later a little whoosh on his phone confirmed that he had received an email. He took a quick look to confirm it was from Walt.

"I'm glad but be careful. This stuff they stole could go for big money on the black market. Big enough to kill for," Walt warned.

His gut clenched at the thought Piper was in such serious danger. No matter, he intended to stick to her like white on rice and keep her safe.

"Roger that, Walt. I'll keep you posted on what happens," he said and swiped to end the call.

He tucked the phone into his back jeans pocket and walked into the living room where Piper waited, green eyes wide in anticipation.

"It was your friend with info, wasn't it?"

# Chapter Seventeen

Her heart pounded so hard in her chest, so loudly, that she couldn't hear what he said next. Laying her hand over her heart, she said, "I'm sorry. Could you repeat what you said?"

"The Marines think that the relics were stolen from Iraq, but that David had nothing to do with it."

"Nothing?" she said, needing the reassurance about what she had known about her husband anyway.

"Nothing. His squad found the relics while on a mission and David reported that to his superiors. They contacted the Iraqi authorities so that the items could be recovered, but they disappeared before they could get there," Shane said and came to sit beside her.

"They're still missing?" she asked and searched Shane's features while he answered.

"They went missing after David was killed in action. The Marines suspected two members of David's squad but couldn't prove it. But they were AWOL for a few days—"

"To steal the relics?"

Shane shrugged and his lips tightened into a grim line. "Possibly. Again, they couldn't prove it, but they had enough to dishonorably discharge the two Marines. My friend sent me the documents but warned that they were heavily redacted. I'd like to print them if I can."

"Sure. Send them to me."

With a few quick swipes he did as she asked and when she got them, she opened the PDFs and printed them. He hopped up from the sofa, hurried over to take the papers from the printer and came back to spread the documents on the coffee table.

*Shane's friend hadn't been wrong about the redaction*, Piper thought, staring at heavy streaks of black across most of the documents. As they read through what they could, the main things they could confirm were what squad they had belonged to, the leader of their squad—David—and the dates when the soldiers had gone AWOL. But luckily, they also had the names of the squad members to turn over to the police.

Piper ran her fingers over the writing on the paper. "David was the leader of this squad. And these dates," she said, running her fingers over a line in the report. "These dates are immediately after David died."

Shane nodded. "They are. It's probably when they decided to go back and take the relics."

Piper waved her hands in a stop gesture. "But someone thinks David had the relics. And they seem to think he sent them to me."

"They do," Shane said and exhaled a long breath. "We need to call Jasper PD and fill them in on all this. Maybe they'll be able to use it to identify who might be behind what's happening."

Piper nodded in agreement. "We need to do that. Maybe we should take this to them?"

"I think that's a good idea."

AVA AND BRADY had been working a late shift away from headquarters, but at their arrival with the information, they'd called in Lieutenant Avery and Jason to sit and review the materials.

As Margaret had read through the materials, she'd said, "The names will help, especially if one of them has a criminal record. If they do, we may be able to use our partial fingerprint and DNA evidence to confirm if it's one of these two individuals."

Satisfied that the officers were doing all they could, he and Piper had returned home.

It was late by the time they got back, but the dogs had needed to be walked. Thankfully the rain had stopped and since he hadn't wanted to leave Piper alone, they took the dogs out together. They did a short loop to the end of the block and back and it was enough for the dogs to relieve themselves.

Inside the house, Piper and he unleashed the dogs and did an awkward little dance as they said good-night. When he went to brush a quick kiss on her lips, she turned her face and he ended up skimming her cheek. Her soft, warm cheek that sported a bright flush of color from his actions.

"Good night," she stammered and raced off to her bedroom, taking Chipper with her. As she closed the door, he walked down the hall to the spare bedroom, Decoy tagging along beside him, clearly happy to be with him.

"You're a good boy," he said and rubbed Decoy's floppy gold-brown ears.

It seemed like a hint of a smile passed across Decoy's mouth before he barked a reply.

"I missed you," he said, but didn't close the door to the bedroom. He wanted to be able to hear if anything was amiss and if so, to be able to deal with it free of any obstacles.

With a quick visit to the bathroom, he got ready for bed, and once he was settled, Decoy jumped up and settled in beside him.

He fell asleep quickly, tired as he was after two sleepless nights and the roller-coaster ride of emotions that both he and Piper had been on.

But when the nightmare came this time, it was different. There was still dust and debris threatening to choke him, but now there was something else. Piper's voice, calling to him.

He fought against the weight on his chest, using almost superhuman strength to lift the rubble off him so he could find Piper in the debris. She was yards away, trapped beneath chunks of concrete and twisted rebar.

"Piper," he called out and reached for her.

She said his name and lifted her hand. Even with the distance between them, he imagined the touch of her hand on his bare chest.

"Shane," he heard, close to his ear as a light weight pressed on him, not as ephemeral as before.

He flailed his arm, trying to knock away that weight, but her voice was louder now. More insistent. "Shane. Wake up, Shane."

Piper blocked his arm and took hold of his hand as he sat up in bed, bare-chested. His scars, both emotional and physical, revealed to her.

"You were having a nightmare," she said and soothed her hand across chest. His skin was damp and chilled from the night air.

"I'm okay," he said, but when his gaze focused and settled on her, he cupped her cheek, almost as if to confirm she was really there.

"You're okay. Everything is okay," she said, trying to reassure him.

Shane rubbed his head, as if trying to dispel the last remnants of the nightmare. He looked away for the briefest moment before settling his gaze on her once more.

"It was different this time," he said and ran his thumb along her chin and the slight dimple there.

She squinted, trying to figure it out, but couldn't. "How was it different?"

"You were in my nightmare," he said, shocking her.

She laid a hand on her chest and squeaked out, "Me. I was in it?"

"You, Piper. You were there, trapped. I was trying to reach you, but I couldn't," he said.

"I'm here, Shane," she said.

"You are," he said and wrapped an arm around her waist and drew her close. As he lay down, he took her with him, and she ended up lying along his length.

His body was so hard beneath hers, calling to the woman who hadn't experienced emotions like this since her husband's death. But as she inched up to meet his lips with hers, she knew it was about more than physical longing. Shane had breached the walls of her heart and she could no longer deny what she was feeling.

She kissed him, moving her mouth along his. Taking in his breath as if she needed it to breathe. Dipping her tongue in to taste him because she wanted to know everything about this strong and caring man.

As he cupped her breast through the thin fabric of her nightshirt, her nipple beaded against his palm. Her breast heavy with need, she covered his hand and pressed it to her, moaned when he tweaked her hard nipple with his fingers.

HIS BREATH EXPLODED from his chest at the sound of her needy moan and the feel of her breast against his palm, beneath his fingers. The softness of her belly cradled his erection and he wanted nothing more than to strip off her thin cotton nightshirt and make love to her, but not like this.

Not when their emotions were running high from the danger threatening Piper's life and his. He had no doubt that if the intruder needed to get to Piper, he'd kill Shane to do it.

"Shane?" Piper asked and leaned a hand on his chest to look at him in the dim light of the room.

"I… I care for you, Piper. I really do, but things are too unsettled now. We're both not thinking straight."

Her eyes widened at his words, and she scrambled off him, but stood by the bed for a halting second. "I care for you, too."

Then she burst from the room, Chipper barking and hopping up and down as she chased after Piper.

Her door slammed shut, but he could hear Piper's

muffled crying, or at least he thought he did, through the wall separating them.

Decoy barked, but it almost seemed like a condemnation of what he'd done.

"Down, Decoy," he said and gestured to the floor beside the bed.

The dog didn't obey. He just sat there, staring at him.

"Down, Decoy," he repeated more sharply.

The dog barked again, but did as he said, his gaze still lifted to Shane's in accusation.

He flipped onto his side, grabbed his pillow and used it to silence Piper's crying and the sight of Decoy's silent condemnation.

Little by little he finally relaxed and tossed aside the pillow. Listened to the silence of the night, broken only by the sound of the mockingbird he'd heard days earlier.

A mockingbird mocking him and the sense of honor that was keeping him from the only woman in his life he'd ever cared about this deeply.

But he'd lived his life with that code of honor intact and he intended it to stay that way.

When this was all over, he'd know whether or not Piper and he were truly meant to be together or if this was just a result of the danger threatening their lives.

THE MORNING WAS chilly in more ways than one, Piper thought.

Breakfast was peppered with curt one-word answers, but at least Shane looked like he had gotten a little more sleep.

They hurriedly finished the quick meal of scrambled eggs and toast, cleaned up and were on their way to the DCA. When they arrived, another car was already parked across from Emma's ranch house.

"Marie's here. She's our vet. I hope nothing's wrong," she said and quickly hopped out of Shane's pickup.

She rushed toward the DCA offices and barn, fearing the worst, but a second later Marie and Emma walked out of the DCA offices, laughing and chatting amiably.

Shane came to her side just as Emma and Marie joined her in the middle of the parking area. "Shane, this is Dr. Marie Beaumont, our vet."

He shook her hand and said, "Shane Adler. Piper's been training my dog and me."

Decoy went to Marie's side, sniffed and then sat at her feet, waiting for her attention. "You're a smart boy, aren't you?" Marie said and playfully rubbed his ears.

"Everything's okay, right?" Piper asked just to confirm.

Emma jerked a hand in Marie's direction. "Someone brought a stray pregnant dog to Marie, but she doesn't have room in her kennels so she asked if we would take care of her."

*And Emma would never say no to any animal or person in trouble*, Piper thought.

"We'll keep a good eye on her," Piper said, and Emma seconded it. "We'll call if there are any complications during the whelping."

"Whelping?" Shane asked, confused by the term.

Marie smiled and explained. "It's what you call it when you deliver a litter of puppies."

"She's that pregnant?" Shane asked, arching a brow.

"She's that pregnant," the vet said with a laugh, the

laughter reaching up into her blue eyes. She was a beautiful woman with dark brown, slightly wavy hair that just brushed her shoulders. Of average height, she had a toned, runner's kind of body that said she was physically active.

"We've done it before, Shane. No need to worry," Piper said and laid a hand on his arm as if to comfort him.

"Good to know because Decoy is the first pet I've ever had," he admitted.

Marie peered at him, as if to size him up. "Military?"

He nodded. "Military. Hard to have a pet."

"I get it. Anyway, I have to get back. I have some patients coming in later today," Marie said and with a wave, she walked to her car, got in and pulled away from the DCA.

"Where's our pregnant patient?" Piper asked.

"The indoor kennels, only…" Emma hesitated, and it was clear something was up.

"Come take a look," she said, and they walked with her to the indoor kennel where a very pregnant dog was resting comfortably on a bed in one of the kennels.

"This is a stray? It looks like a purebred basenji. Not the kind of dog we see around here," she said and bent to scratch the dog's ears, earning a grateful lick from the little pointy-eared dog. She had a short red-and-white coat and a tightly curled tail and even he could see that this was not a mutt.

"That's what I thought. I'm going to call Jasper PD to see if anyone has reported one that's missing or stolen," Emma said and went to her office to make the call.

"It's a beautiful dog," Shane said and followed Piper out of the DCA offices to the agility course.

Piper's brow furrowed but relaxed as she said, "Beautiful and very smart. But we have our own smart pups, right?"

"Right," he said, and Piper immediately went to work with Decoy, putting him through the paces on the agility course the first time. Once Decoy had finished, she turned it over to him and he guided Decoy through all the obstacles over and over. Decoy did each run without any hesitation or faults.

"Good boy. Good boy," he said and rewarded Decoy with treats and a body rub.

"He is a good boy. I know it's going to be a little muddy, but I'd like to take him out on the trail. Just give me a moment to hide some things."

She left him on the trail and went into the DCA's offices and he took advantage to put Decoy through another run on the agility course. He caught a glimpse of Piper as she walked between the offices and the barn to head to the trail. It made him uneasy to think about her out there with only Chipper for protection.

With a low whistle and hand signal to Decoy, they hurried to the space between the two buildings where he could keep an eye on Piper as she walked down the trail. He could see her hiding things here and there along the path and when she returned, she rolled her eyes at the sight of him standing there.

"I'm safe here," she said and held her hands wide to the area around them.

He didn't want to worry her, so he agreed despite his misgivings. "You are safe here."

One reddish brow shot upward to let him know she didn't believe him, but she only said, "Let's see what Decoy can do on the trail."

## Chapter Eighteen

Decoy did wonderfully during the session, finding Emma's work gloves and knit cap as well as several other hot dogs. Except for one that Chipper beat him to at the end, possibly because by then Decoy's belly was full.

"Chipper, that's not for you," Piper said as Chipper jogged away with the hot dog in her mouth.

"Smart dog," Shane added, chuckling at the sight of Piper chasing Chipper. When she caught the squat little puppy, she hauled her up into her arms, laughing. Her green eyes were the color of emeralds and glittering with happiness. He was relieved that her upset from the night before had been chased away by the antics of the dogs. Or maybe she was better at hiding her feelings than he thought.

He liked seeing her like this, free of the worry that had plagued her during the last few weeks.

When the puppy gobbled up the last of the hot dog, Piper set him down. "Maybe I should be teaching Chipper to do search and rescue."

Although their focus had been on Decoy during their training, Chipper had been obedient and learned many of the same commands. Not as quickly as Decoy, but eventually the little pup had learned.

"She's a good dog," he said again and bent to rub Chipper's head when the puppy came over, seemingly aware that he was talking about her.

"She is. Come here, Chipper," Piper said, and the little dog complied and sat at Piper's feet, waiting for the next command. Piper rewarded her with a treat and when she straightened, she said, "I guess we can call it a day. It's almost five."

"Sounds good." He strolled beside her, their pace slow to enjoy the beautiful late afternoon sun. The dogs played together along the trail.

"They're good friends," Piper said, grinning at the sight of the two mismatched dogs tussling over a branch. Decoy was at least a foot taller, his body thicker with his Lab/hound background. Chipper had the short legs of the corgi, and her body wasn't as muscular despite the pit bull in her.

"They are friends. Or maybe it's love," he teased and wanted to bite his tongue as Piper shot a quick look at him out of the corner of her eye.

"Love, huh?" she said, her tone a mix of playful and serious. Her gaze saying her words might be more than about the dogs.

With a side-eyed glance, he said, "Maybe."

The dogs ran ahead between the two buildings and as they turned the corner, Ava and Brady were standing there.

Piper waved at them, and the two officers returned the wave and approached.

"We went by your place and when you weren't home, we figured you'd be here," Ava said.

"You guessed right," Piper said and quickly added, "Do you have something for us?"

Ava shot a quick look at Brady, who did a slow nod to confirm she should continue. As the lieutenant, he had the higher rank and was likely in charge along with Lieutenant Avery.

Ava pulled her notebook out of her jacket pocket, flipped through a few pages and then began her report. "We reviewed the papers you sent us and tracked down the two men. Buck Devare is clean as a whistle. He's been working as a clerk in his family's business. Married. One child."

She flipped to the next page and said, "The second man has a criminal record. Josh Parker. Came back from Afghanistan and a few months later ended up in county jail on a misdemeanor assault and battery charge. He's out in six months, but not long after that he's back in jail for second-degree robbery. Broke into a liquor store in the middle of the night. Got two years in prison for that one."

"All of that was in California. We got his fingerprints from those crimes and even though our print was only partial, there are a lot of points of identification," Brady added to her report.

"What about the DNA on the cigarette butts?" Shane asked, hoping that the DNA would be the final nail to confirm it was Parker who was responsible for the burglary.

"We should have our analysis back in the next few days. Second-degree robbery is a felony in California so his DNA was collected and hopefully is in CODIS so we can see if it's a match," Ava explained.

Piper glanced at him and then back to the officers. "That's all good, then, isn't it?"

"Oceanside PD went by Parker's California apartment, but he wasn't there. The manager hasn't seen him in weeks. Probably because he's past due on his rent. Until we have him in custody, we all need to stay alert. In the meantime, we've put out a BOLO on Parker," Brady said and tapped a finger to the brim of the baseball cap with the Jasper PD's emblem. "We should get going."

"We'll keep you advised," Ava said, and the two officers turned and walked back to their police cruiser.

As they drove away, Piper said, "That's all pretty good, right?" She shot a quick look up at him.

Hands on his hips, he gazed toward the cruiser as it moved down the long drive of the DCA and turned off to head back in the direction of Piper's home. "It is, but like Brady said, we need to stay alert until they can locate Parker."

Piper's shoulders slumped at his comment.

He laid his arm across her back and drew her against him. "It's going to be okay."

She worried her lower lip with her teeth and nodded, but it was halfhearted. "It will be."

"Let's get cleaned up and make it a night. Maybe call Emma to see if she's free. Try to put this all behind us," he said and playfully bumped his hip against hers.

"I like that idea."

THE BREWERY WAS PACKED, not unexpected for a Friday night in Jasper, especially with the warmer late April weather. It wasn't unusual to have the first small wave of tourists coming to see the wildflowers or head up into the higher elevations for a last blast of snow before it melted. Come the middle of May in a few weeks and they'd start to see more of the hikers, fishermen and rafters along the Salmon River.

Even with the crowd, they were quickly seated at a small table at a spot far from the bar, making it a little quieter so they could talk.

When Piper had phoned Emma earlier to invite her to dinner, she had filled in her friend on the report that Ava and Brady had provided. She had hoped that by doing so the three of them could avoid talk of the break-in during dinner and have a fun night.

*The three of us*, Piper thought, wondering why Shane had decided to include Emma. Granted, she was the owner of the DCA and the person Gonzo had recommended for Decoy's training. But she had been the one primarily doing the training, although Emma had dropped by on occasion to see what was up and offer advice behind the scenes.

*OMG, am I jealous of Emma?* she thought with a start.

*No way*, she thought as the waitress came over to hand them menus. It was just that she had thought that if Shane was asking her out…

*Whoa, not a date*, the little voice reminded.

Not a date because Emma was here and maybe that was exactly what Shane had wanted after that kiss the other night. A kiss that had rocked her and made her wish for things that weren't possible. It had upset her, but the training and the dogs had helped restore some calm to her battered emotions. But she couldn't ignore that it would be way too dangerous for the two of them to go to dinner alone, maybe have a beer and then go home to sleep in the same house.

*Maybe in the same bed*, she thought and felt the heat of color bloom across her cheeks.

"Piper? Did you hear us?" Emma asked, hooking a finger at the top of Piper's menu to lower it slightly.

"No, sorry," she said, and the heat ignited into a blaze, making her want to cover her cheeks with her hands but that would only be way more embarrassing.

Emma scrutinized her carefully. "You feeling okay?"

Her gaze jumped to Shane's for a split second, and it was impossible to miss the humor there. He covered his mirth by coughing into his hand and after a hot second, he said, "I guess we got too much sun out on the trail."

Emma looked from him to Piper. "Sure. Sun. We asked if you wanted to share a blooming onion."

*Onion. Totally unromantic. Perfect.* "That would be great."

"Great. I love onion," Shane said, and one dark eyebrow shot up in challenge.

*Ignore him*, she told herself, and luckily, the rest of the night passed without incident.

Burgers were eaten. Beer was consumed, although not too much since both Shane and Emma were driving. As they were exiting, they ran into Tashya and Jason, who were arriving for a date, and Brady and his best friend, Officer Dillon Diaz.

After hugs and goodbyes, Emma peeled off at the curb to go to her car and she and Shane walked to his pickup. As she was hopping up into the cab, a blue pickup slowly drove by, making the hairs on her neck rise. She tried to get a look at the driver, but the windows were tinted, and he had a baseball cap pulled down low.

She inched up, trying to see the license plate, but he was already too far away.

"Something wrong?" Shane asked when she finally sat in the passenger seat.

"A blue pickup went by, and it freaked me out a little," she confessed.

"Where did it go?" he asked and quickly started the engine.

She pointed down the street. "That way."

But as he pulled out, she could see that the pickup had already turned off West Second and was no longer visible. "It's gone," she said, dejected.

Shane did a quick look in her direction. "Did you get a license plate number?"

She shook her head. "No. He was too far away, and it was too dark."

Shane reached out and stroked her arm. "Don't worry. We will catch him."

She wished she could be as sure. The happiness she'd been feeling after their carefree dinner had been dimmed by the appearance of the blue pickup.

The ride home was quiet, the cab filled with the sound of the tires on the road and, as they stopped, the rustle of the wind through branches, as well as a mockingbird that seemed to have made her yard home.

She hopped out of the pickup and Shane was immediately there, his big hand at the small of her back. The touch was possessive. Intimate. Reminding her of where they had almost gone the other night. But she had to push those thoughts aside.

As she went to unlock the door, Shane reached around and laid a hand on hers. "Let me."

He took the key from her hand and stepped past her to open the door and disarm the alarm. "Please wait here," he said and walked into the house to take a quick look around, which she could have easily done in her small two-bedroom ranch.

"All clear," he said and came back into the living room, Chipper and Decoy chasing after him. "I guess we should take these two for a quick walk."

"Sounds good," she said and took Chipper's leash as Shane handed it to her.

They armed the alarm and locked up for the short walk, which seemed like overkill, but as Ava and Brady had warned, they had to stay alert.

The night was quiet with a slight nippiness. The mockingbird was trilling his trio of repetitive notes, making her ask, "Do you think he ever gets tired of repeating the same thing?"

SHANE LAUGHED. "Sometimes the same thing is a good thing," he said, thinking of all the times he would have wished for that while on patrol in Afghanistan. Just a moment of quiet. Of peace, like the peace he felt here, with her and the dogs, which was like a slice of heaven.

"I know what you mean. When Emma first asked me to come here, I worried I'd be bored, but there's something about the routine and nights like this... It's wonderful." She stopped as Chipper went to relieve herself by the side of the road.

Decoy joined her a second later and Shane quickly scooped the dogs' messes.

"Thanks. I always wonder if aliens came to earth and saw us scooping, they'd think the dogs were our masters," she said with a laugh.

Shane chuckled and did a little shake of his head. "Until they watched a cat and realized who was truly in charge."

Piper laughed even harder and louder. "OMG, so true. My mom had a cat that totally ruled our house."

He loved the sound of her laugh. The way her eyes crinkled at the edges and darkened to a jewel-like green. Her full lips, a lovely rose color against the creaminess of her skin.

She was so beautiful. So strong and smart and he thought he might love her, which brought him to a grinding halt by the side of the road.

She stopped as well, stumped by his action. A furrow marred the smooth skin of her brow as she peered at him. "Something wrong?"

Everything, he wanted to say, because things had gotten way too complicated. "No. Just enjoying the night," he lied and started walking again, Decoy beside him, sniffing along the edges of the road.

Piper fell into step beside him, Chipper slipping in between them to be closer to Decoy. It created space between them, which was welcome considering where his thoughts had been going.

At the door they repeated their earlier routine: disarming the alarm, checking the house, locking up and resetting the alarm. Security being paramount until they caught Parker and confirmed that he had been the one who had trashed Piper's home and stolen her wedding rings.

Side by side, they walked through the living room to the hallway leading to the bedrooms. Piper took the lead down the hall, pausing by the door to her room, where she faced him.

"Good night, Shane," she said, but her tone was hesitant. Bordering on inviting, but it brought back memories of the other night and his hesitation at taking this relationship further. But he didn't want to keep on denying that he wished there could be more with her.

He took an uncertain step closer and when she didn't back away, he bent and kissed her. Not like their fleeting first kiss or the more heated one from the other night. This was a kiss of invitation and promise. Tender at first, but growing deeper as they stood there, kissing over and over until he finally closed the distance and laid a hand at her waist to urge her closer.

Her breasts were soft against his chest. Her hips mobile when she shifted them against his erection, but as much as he wanted to take this to the next level, he couldn't until he was sure of himself and what he could offer her.

Because of that, he tempered his kiss and stepped away the tiniest bit, but it was enough.

The kiss ended as tentatively as it began, with a lingering brush of their lips and a sigh that was loud in the quiet of the night.

He moved back another step, enough to see her face.

The slight flush on her cheeks. Her eyes, slightly dazed and dark. Her lips, still moist from their kiss.

"Sweet dreams, Piper," he said and didn't wait for her reply, thinking it best to go to his own room before he made a big mistake.

Her "good night" chased him down the hall as did the sound of her door closing.

But as he had the night before, he left his open. He changed quickly and slipped beneath the sheets, Decoy at the side of the bed. Pillowing his hands beneath his head, he stared at the ceiling and mentally reviewed all the information that Walt had provided as well as that from the two police officers. Josh Parker seemed like a piece of work, and it worried him to think that someone like that might be after Piper and whatever Parker thought might be in her possession.

*Relics*, he thought and tried to imagine what they might be and where they could be hiding.

He'd heard his share about things like that when he'd done a short stint in Iraq. Between the American military activity and the advent of ISIS, quite a number of Iraqi museums had suffered damage and looting. But how could someone manage to slip anything like that past Customs or the other authorities? And why did Parker think that Piper had it? Was it because the relics were gone when he and Devare had gone back for them, making them think that Lambert had somehow taken them before he was killed?

Only whoever Walt had spoken to was sure Lambert wasn't involved, which left Parker and Devare as the likely suspects, even if the military investigators hadn't been able to prove it.

Piper and he had looked through everything. Whatever these relics were, Piper didn't have them.

But that didn't matter to Parker, and because of that, they'd have to continue to be careful.

## Chapter Nineteen

Piper raised her face to the morning sun, enjoying the warmth of it on her face.

There was less of a chill in the mid-April air, but snow still frosted the highest elevations on the mountain. But today's warmth was a sign that in another couple of weeks, that snow would melt and send water cascading down into the Salmon River, bringing waves of rafters to enjoy the rushing waters.

"Penny for your thoughts," Shane said from beside her. They were walking the dogs before packing them up for the ride to that morning's training at the DCA.

She pointed to the mountains. "Snow will be gone soon." *And so will you*, she thought. It was his last week of training before he went off to work with the search and rescue group in Montana.

With a side-eyed glance, he said, "Sun feels great. Might be nice to go for a hike today."

She stopped and eyeballed him. "Are you suggesting we play hooky today?"

He held his hands up as if in pleading. "We've been working hard for weeks. Things have been quiet for a few days. Why not take a little time off? We could do a quick training session, get a picnic lunch and then take a hike. Maybe even dinner."

They had been working hard and things had been quiet. It had been nearly a week since anything had happened around her house and things between her and Shane... Things had been good. Companionable, not that companionable was what either of them wanted.

There could be no denying the tension between them. The desire that they'd kept banked night after night as he'd kiss her good-night and then head to the spare bedroom.

Maybe a long hike in the woods was just what they needed to dispel that tension and desire.

"Sure, why not?"

JOSH HAD KEPT his distance for a week, hoping things with the cops would die down if nothing else happened. Certain that the police were looking for him, he'd trimmed his hair to a high-and-tight buzz cut and dyed it blond to look different from his driver's license photo.

He'd also left the blue pickup he'd stolen in McCall, a town about an hour south of Jasper, exchanging it for a white Jeep that might handle better in the slushy snow surrounding the mountain cabin where he'd been hiding out. The cabin had been in rough shape, clearly unused for some time, but it hadn't taken much to make it habitable and a place where he could hold Lambert's widow until she told him where she'd hidden the relics.

Now it was time to start watching again. To wait for the perfect time to grab Piper and get what he was owed.

Lambert had screwed everything up for him big-time. He'd planned on selling the treasures to finally have the kind of life most people only dreamed of.

But then Lambert had been killed, the relics had gone missing, and the Marines had come down hard on them for being AWOL. And unlike Buck, his life had done nothing but go downhill once he'd gotten home.

No one in the military-oriented town had wanted to hire someone with a dishonorable discharge. A fight over some comments about that discharge had landed him in jail. That had made it even harder to get employed and he'd resorted to stealing to put food on the table and a roof over his head. He just hadn't planned on the roof over his head to be in prison.

He wasn't going to let that happen again.

That's why he was hanging back, waiting for the right moment.

As he looked through the binoculars, he watched them hiking the trail along the river's edge, looking way too happy and lovey-dovey. Especially since the big guy had basically moved into her house.

Made life way harder for him, but he'd find a way to grab her.

*I just have to be patient*, he told himself and continued watching them.

PIPER TRUDGED ALONG the trail, Shane right behind her. As she walked, she pointed out things along the path. "See that stand of aspens over there?" she said, and Shane followed the line of her arm to gaze at the large stand of trees halfway up a nearby hillside. "They call that stand a 'clone' because the aspens grow by sprouting from their roots so they all have the same DNA.

In the fall they'll be an amazing gold color against the evergreens."

The trees were a bright spring green now, still obvious among the darker shades of the evergreens. As he watched, a bald eagle flew off from the branches and swooped down toward the river along the trail they were hiking.

"Beautiful sight," he said, but as he followed the path of the eagle, his gaze skipped to Piper and he thought, *Even more beautiful.*

"I hope to see that gold," he said, but then wished he had bit his tongue because he wouldn't be in Jasper in the fall.

She slowly tilted her head up to meet his gaze. "I hope you do, too."

But then she was quickly plowing ahead along the trail, until she held her hand up to stop them. He was about to say something, only she held an index finger to her lips to quiet him. "Shh. Mule deer."

Far ahead of them, a mule deer was slaking its thirst along the river's edge. Its black-tipped tail and large ears, similar to a mule's, were different from the white-tailed deer he'd seen growing up in Pennsylvania and around the training center in California.

The deer must have sensed them. It raised its head to stare in their direction and then bolted toward the hillside.

"They stay down in the valley during the winter but will head up to the higher elevations during the summer," Piper explained.

"Is there much hunting in this area?" he asked, tracking the deer as long as he could until he lost sight of it in a thick stand of trees.

Sadness filtered into her gaze, animal lover that she was. "The mule deer population is down in this area, so Fish and Game issued fewer permits in the hopes of building their numbers."

"Sounds like they're trying to protect them," Shane said, and Piper nodded and offered up a reluctant smile.

"They are. Idaho Fish and Game also operate nearly two dozen hatcheries to raise all kinds of fish in order to stock our rivers and lakes, including sockeye salmon, which are endangered. Luckily they've had some success with steelhead and other kinds of salmon."

"When I was growing up, we had a small pond near our house. Town used to stock it with trout and my dad and I would go fishing," Shane said, smiling as memories of those idyllic times streamed back.

"Looks like they were good memories. We could try some salmon fishing later this week if you want. Catch and release, though," Piper said and started moving along the trail again.

"I'd like that." They hadn't gone more than half a mile when they caught sight of someone fly-fishing along the edges of the river. He waved as he saw them, and they waved back and kept on walking until they hit a section of the river that was shallow enough to traverse.

They crossed over and his storm boots kept his feet dry, but there was no denying the cold of the water streaming down the river. The rocks were slippery and as Piper wavered a little, he reached out to keep her steady. A glint of something high up on the hillside caught his eye, like sun bouncing off glass or metal.

*Like someone watching, maybe?* he thought and hurried Piper across the stream and into the protection of the trees and underbrush on the opposite edge of the riverbank.

The earlier happiness he'd been feeling vanished, replaced by watchfulness as they did the walk back to his pickup.

"You okay?" she asked as they neared his vehicle, obviously sensing the change in his mood.

Not wanting to worry her, he said, "Just a little tired. It's been a long time since I've done a hike this long."

She eyed him up and down and did a little shake of her head. "Not like you're out of shape."

He faked it, reaching up to rub his injured shoulder. "Acts up at the weirdest times."

Her wrinkled brow said that she wasn't quite buying it, but he wasn't going to push it because he'd never been a good liar. Actually, he'd never been any kind of liar.

"Time to go home, then," she said and got into the pickup after he unlocked the doors.

"Maybe we can stop in Jasper for an early dinner?" he said as he pulled out and drove along the road in the direction of town, heading west before then heading north toward Piper's house and the DCA.

"You're still hungry after that lunch we ate?" Piper said with a laugh.

The roast beef sandwiches, salads and cookies that Millard's had packed for their picnic had been satisfying, but if someone was watching them, a stop in a more populated area like Jasper might make for a safe haven until he could confirm if they were being followed.

"Fresh air always makes me hungry," he said and looked in the rearview mirror to see if anyone was behind them. Two cars way in the distance, but no blue pickup.

It had probably been nothing on the hillside.

They had barely gone another few miles and were still a goodly distance from Jasper when he spied a woman and dog lying on the side of the road. She started waving her hand in the air as they neared, and Shane had no choice but to pull over and see what was happening.

PIPER HOPPED DOWN from Shane's pickup and raced over to the woman and dog.

The woman's right leg was at an awkward angle and the dog was bleeding and breathing heavily.

Piper kneeled beside the dog and laid a hand on its side, trying to gauge the extent of its injuries. The dog's muscles trembled beneath her hand as the woman said, "We were hiking back to our car when someone sideswiped us. My dog took the brunt of the hit."

Shane had squatted beside the woman to check out her leg. "It looks broken. We can try to get you in the bed of the pickup."

The woman shook her head. "My hip, too. Something's wrong there, but I can't feel anything. My leg... hip, everything feels numb."

Piper exchanged a worried look with Shane. "We'll call for help," she said, then whipped out her phone to dial 911 and gave them the information on their location and situation.

"My dog. His name is Longmire. He's hurt bad. You've got to get him help," the woman said and tried to reach for him, but screamed as she moved, the numbness possibly starting to wear off.

"Lie down and relax. We'll take care of Longmire for you," Shane said and urged the woman to lie down. He took off his jacket and placed it over the woman to keep her warm.

With a tilt of his head, he urged Piper away from the pair.

In a low whisper that only he could hear, she said, "The dog needs immediate care or he might not make it."

"We can't leave her alone," Shane said and shot a quick glance at the woman.

Piper tilted her head in the direction of his pickup. "You can load him into the bed, and I'll take him to Marie's."

He shook his head. "It's not safe for you to go alone. Let me take him."

"It's not more than ten miles and you don't know the way to the vet," she said, but he shook his head again and she narrowed her eyes to scrutinize him. "Is there something you're not telling me?"

## Chapter Twenty

Shane peered up and down the road and Piper did the same, but there was no one in the vicinity.

"No, there's nothing wrong, just… Keep an eye out. We haven't found Parker yet," he said.

"I will keep an eye out, I promise," she said and held her hand out for his keys.

He handed them to her. "I'll go get the dog. There's a blanket in the back seat you can lay out to make him more comfortable."

She opened the door, reached in and got the blanket, which she spread in the bed of the pickup. Shane walked over with the dog, who was whining with pain. She ran a hand over his side, trying to calm him. "Easy, boy. You're going to be okay."

"Call me as soon as you get there," he said and brushed a kiss across her cheek.

She nodded. "I will."

Shane hurried back to the woman to take care of her, and Piper rushed to the pickup and took off down the road.

She hadn't gone more than a mile or so when she

spotted the ambulance on the way to where Shane waited with the woman.

Barely half a dozen miles later, she caught sight in the rearview mirror of a white Jeep barreling toward her quickly. Too quickly.

Slowing, she pulled over slightly to let them pass since they were in such a rush. The wheel jerked in her hand a little as the tires hit the softer dirt along the edge of the road.

The Jeep rushed past her, but when she pulled back onto the road, the Jeep suddenly veered in front of her, blocking the way across the street.

She jerked to a rough stop, hands gripping the steering wheel tightly as the driver of the vehicle got out.

He had on a baseball cap and sunglasses hid his eyes, but she didn't need to see them to know something wasn't right about him.

She put the car in Reverse, intending to get away, when his hand whipped up and he trained a gun in her direction.

"I wouldn't do that, Piper. I'm an excellent shot."

SHANE STOOD BY impatiently as the EMTs worked on the woman, stabilizing her for transport to Jasper Memorial, which luckily wasn't all that far from town. Nearly fifteen minutes had gone by since Piper had driven off, and an uneasy feeling filled his gut.

*She should be in Jasper by now*, he thought. Maybe she was helping the vet with the dog. Maybe Marie wasn't there, and Piper was waiting for her. *Maybe, maybe, maybe*, he thought, wanting to get to Jasper and Piper, only he didn't have a ride.

Ava and Brady pulled up in their cruiser minutes later and there was still no call from Piper.

"Shane," Ava said and both she and Brady dipped their heads in greeting.

"Ava. Brady," he said and glanced back toward the EMTs as they finally loaded the woman onto the gurney and walked with her toward the ambulance.

"Where's Piper? We thought she was with you when she called in the accident," Ava said and looked all around.

"Lady had a dog that was badly hurt. Piper took the pickup to take him to Marie in town."

"What can you tell us about what happened here?" Brady asked.

One of the EMTs called out, "We're taking her in, Lieutenant Nichols. You can meet us at Jasper Memorial."

"We'll meet you there shortly," Ava responded.

"Shane?" Brady asked again.

"Piper and I were driving back to Jasper when we saw the woman and the dog on the side of the road. We stopped and she told us that a car had sideswiped them. We called it in to get her help. Piper took the dog, and she hasn't called me yet from the vet's," Shane said.

Brady did a quick look at his watch. "She should have been to Marie's by now."

"Can we get going?" Shane asked and pointed to the cruiser.

"Sure," Ava said, and they rushed to the police car and hurried off, Shane in the back seat, nervously bouncing his legs while Ava drove.

"How long ago did she leave?" Brady asked.

"Too long. At least twenty minutes. Maybe more," he said and then something hit him. "Didn't you pass her on your way here?"

Ava shook her head and met his gaze in the rearview mirror. "We were just coming back from McCall. We got a call that they'd found the blue pickup—"

"The one Parker was driving?" Shane pressed.

"The one we believe Parker was driving. We went to check it out and see what other information we could get," Brady said.

Which meant Parker was driving some other kind of vehicle. Maybe even one of the ones he'd seen behind them after they'd left the trail near the Salmon River.

He mumbled a curse, but then the two officers did as well, making him lean forward to see what was going on.

His pickup. Sitting by the side of the road.

They pulled up next to it.

No sign of Piper and the dog was still in the bed of the pickup.

They hopped out of the cruiser and hurried to the front of his car.

There were signs of a skid mark across the road, as if a car had suddenly stopped in the path of the pickup.

As Shane examined the black marks, he noticed that there were some tire tracks along the softer dirt at the edge of the road. He gestured to them. "Another car. Across the road."

Ava and Brady walked over to the tire tracks to take a look and he joined them. "We saw tire tracks near Piper's house, but something's a little different."

Brady kneeled down for a closer inspection. "Pickup

and Jeep might both use the same tires, but the wheel-bases are different. This isn't a pickup. The wheelbase isn't wide enough. Probably a Jeep. Narrower, but we'll know once we measure and cast the tire impressions."

"But first we need to put a BOLO out for Piper and get some backup to take that dog to the vet," Ava said, then grabbed her radio and called it in.

Shane cursed, loudly and more vehemently as he raked his hand through his hair and paced away from where the two officers were reviewing the scene.

The crime scene.

Parker had grabbed Piper and he wasn't about to just sit there and do nothing.

"We need to get going," he said and moved toward his pickup, but Ava held up a hand to stop him.

"We need to process the scene and do this logically," she said, and while he knew she was right, it didn't make the delay any easier to bear.

"Okay. We do this your way," he said even though he was itching to get moving.

PARKER HAD KNOCKED HER out with the gun butt when she'd stepped out of Shane's car.

Or at least she assumed it was Parker, even though he looked different from the driver's license photo the police had shown them.

She woke up with a gag stuffed in her mouth and se-cured in place with a bandanna. Her wrists were duct-taped behind her back, which made it impossible for her to do anything like reach for the door handle in order to escape.

But her legs were free.

She carefully watched the scenery going by, looking for landmarks that might help her make her way back toward Jasper if she got free.

*Not if, when*, she told herself.

And when she did, she'd have to make her way down the mountain. That much she knew: he was taking her up into the mountains.

It was the growing chill of the air that had roused her into consciousness. The jacket she had worn for the hike was too lightweight for the higher elevations, especially since there was snow on the ground where he was taking them.

Probably one of the many vacation cabins that sometimes sat vacant for weeks, even months depending on the owner's tastes for either skiing, hiking or rafting.

Judging from the silhouette of the mountain crests, he'd kept on going north, but had probably detoured around Jasper to hide from the authorities. That meant he'd also passed by the general vicinity of her home and the DCA.

Hope blossomed that, if she could escape, she could reach either her home or the canine academy.

But as the Jeep slipped on a slushy patch on the road, it warned her that escape on foot could be treacherous. The snow would make footing precarious, and she wasn't properly dressed for any time in the cold.

Another half hour passed, and her arms and shoulders complained from their awkward position pinned behind her.

She was relieved when Parker finally pulled up in front of a log cabin. Not one of the nice vacation places. A ramshackle cabin whose roof looked ready to cave

in on one side. The glass in several windows was broken, but someone had done temporary repairs by tap-
ing plastic over the holes. A small pile of firewood was
haphazardly placed by the front door, but it wouldn't be
enough to last the night.

Parker killed the engine and climbed out of the Jeep.

He yanked her door open and roughly jerked her
from the seat. She stumbled and fell. He lost his grip
on her and she figured this was as good a chance as
any to escape.

Before he could grab her again, she crab-walked
away from him and somehow managed to get to her
feet. But she had only taken a step or two when Parker
tackled her to the ground, the weight of his body driving her breath from her.

Darkness danced around the edges of her periphery
from the lack of air. Pain seared the muscles of her arms
as Parker hauled her to her feet.

"Not smart, Piper. Not smart," he said and half
dragged, half carried her into the cabin, where he sat
her in a chair that creaked and groaned, as if ready to
break. When she tried to rise, he pulled out the pistol
and said, "Don't. I will shoot you."

She peered at the gun and then at Parker. Her heart
galloped in her chest and a cold sweat erupted across
her body, chilling her thanks to the lack of heat in the
cabin. Nodding, she quieted in the chair and sat patiently while Parker duct-taped her feet to the chair legs.
Then he wrapped the tape around her body and the
chair, dimming any hope she had of getting free and
making an escape.

When he was done, he pulled off the bandanna and

took the gag from her mouth, but warned, "Scream and I'll shoot you."

Feigning a bravado she didn't really feel, she said, "If you do, you won't find out what I know about the relics."

A hint of surprise registered on his features before he squinted to examine her features. "Your husband told you about the relics before he died?"

"No. My friend—"

"The big guy. Military I assume?" he said and started pacing in front of her, the gun held, muzzle down, at his side.

Piper didn't see the point in denying it. "Ex-Army. He asked some friends who told him about the relics and your dishonorable discharge for being AWOL."

"That discharge was all a lie. Should have only been some time in the brig and loss of pay. We weren't deserters. We were only gone for a few days."

"Because you were stealing the relics," she challenged.

He whirled to face her, his agitation impossible to miss. His face was a mottled red and he tapped the gun against his thigh repeatedly. "Because your husband had already taken them, and we were trying to figure out where since he was dead."

"David didn't take them. He would never do anything like that," she shot back.

"Saint David. That's what the rest of the squad called him behind his back. Mr. Goody Two-shoes, but when we found the relics, you should have seen his eyes light up. He knew how much they were worth on the black market."

"He didn't take them," she repeated, having no doubt

about her husband's character. She was sad that his men had somehow thought of him disparagingly because he had always spoken highly about the squad under his command.

"Really? You seem to have landed on your feet. Nice house even if it is out here in the boondocks. Where did you get the money, Piper?" He leaned forward and got in her face. "Did you sell the relics?"

She tilted her chin up defiantly and met his gaze, hers never wavering. "Life insurance. David took care of me just like he took care of his men, you included."

Parker blew out a rough laugh and backed away from her. "If he cared he would have let us grab the relics when we found them. But no, he had to report the find and then he stole them." He whirled on her again, the nervous tapping of the gun against his leg heightening her own nervousness since it warned Parker was on the edge.

"He stole them, and you have them," he repeated, a hint of crazy in his voice.

"I don't," she said calmly, hoping to defuse the situation. "You've got the wrong person, Josh. Maybe you should be checking with your buddy Devare. He's the one who seems to have landed on his feet."

"Buck wouldn't do that. Besides, he was looking with me. He got dishonorably discharged just like me," Josh said, leaning in until they were nose to nose and tapping his chest with his free hand. Spittle flew from his lips, some of it landing on her cheek.

"But he ended up with a nice job, a wife and a child, while you ended up in jail and basically homeless. Doesn't sound like much of a friend to me," she said and for a moment, she thought she detected a momentary flicker of doubt. But then he shook his head, as if shaking away the doubt, and stepped away. He went to one corner of the cabin and hauled another rickety chair to the middle of the room, directly opposite her.

He sat down, the hand with the pistol resting on his thigh. "Buck's the best. He wouldn't betray me, but your Saint David... Where are the relics?"

Piper shook her head. "I don't have them. I never had them because David didn't take them," she repeated, her voice steady and unruffled.

Josh looked away and did a quick tilt of his head. "Going to be a long night. Even longer days because you're not leaving until I get the relics."

While the thought of being held for days was scary and painful, since she was slowly losing feeling in her hands from how he'd bound them, she took hope in the fact that he had mentioned her leaving this hovel. Alive. But she also hoped that Shane and the police would find her long before that.

She had expected that Josh would keep on pushing her for answers, but instead he just sat there, watching her. Watching the afternoon sun dim and the shadows of dusk fill the room. She wondered if he was playing some kind of mind game with her but told herself to remain calm.

As it started to get even darker, he rose and brought in the small pile of wood he'd had by the door and placed a few of the logs in a fireplace that still held the remnants of another fire.

"Can't start a fire until it's dark. Don't want them to

see the smoke and know where we are," he explained and rubbed his hand against the cold in the room.

After some cursing and muttering, the first tiny lick of flame was visible and soon he had a small fire going. Very small because it only illuminated a tiny circle of brick in front of the fireplace.

The scrape of metal against the brick drew her attention. He was placing a cooking rack over the flames, obviously intending to prepare a meal. She had no illusions he would share it with her, not that she was hungry. Her stomach was tied up in knots worrying about how long he'd keep her here and what he would do to her if she didn't tell him something about the relics he thought she had.

Despite his earlier words and his actions since taking her, things could change in a heartbeat and not in a good way.

But if she knew one thing about Shane, it was that he would never give up until he found her. He was the kind of man you could depend on. Who would be there for you and who she wanted to be there for her. She intended to tell him that when she could.

## Chapter Twenty-One

Shane paced back and forth across the narrow width of the meeting room where members of the Jasper PD force had gathered together along with Emma to review the evidence they'd amassed and to formulate a plan for finding Piper.

Lieutenants Avery and Nichols, who had already been involved in the case. Officer Callan and rookie Officer Jason Wright. Lieutenant Hoover, the seniormost officer besides Captain Rutledge and the chief, was also present. Hoover was a handsome African American with a muscular build and a sharp brown gaze that seemed to take everything in although he remained silent as his officers provided their reports.

Emma sat beside Hoover, her hands laced together tightly, her fingers white from the pressure. Hoover laid his big hand over Emma's, offering reassurance as he said, "We will find her."

"It's been hours," Emma said, fear making her voice quake.

"Too long," Shane chimed in, earning a hard glance and rebuke from Brady.

"You more than most know how important it is to

not go off half-cocked, Shane. There's a lot of territory to cover and we need to do it sensibly," the officer said.

He bit back a challenge, aware that Brady was right. Injecting calm into his voice, he sat and said, "What is the plan?"

Margaret rose and went to a whiteboard at one end of the room. "We know from the tire tracks left behind that Parker's changed vehicles. The wheelbase was too narrow for a pickup. Based on the wheelbase and tires, we identified it as possibly being a Jeep."

She wrote that down on the whiteboard and Ava chimed in with, "McCall PD confirmed that a red Jeep was taken not far from the location where Parker dumped the blue pickup he stole in Boise."

Margaret added that info along with the license plate number for the stolen red Jeep. She pointed to it and said, "We have a BOLO out for that vehicle."

Lieutenant Hoover stepped into the discussion. "I think we can eliminate that Parker headed back to Mc-Call with Piper. McCall is a nice size, but it would be hard for him to hide now that McCall PD will be looking for that Jeep. He also wouldn't head into Jasper for the same reason."

"Agreed," Margaret said, and all the officers seated around the table were nodding when another officer poked his head into the room.

"Looks like you called in the cavalry, Hoover," the man said and stepped into the room, hands on his hips. The nameplate on his black shirt said "Rutledge."

Shane recognized the name from some of Emma and Piper's earlier discussions about the man and his disdain for the K-9 programs they ran. He was a handsome man with light brown hair and a blue-eyed gaze that flitted, almost disparagingly, over the people gathered in the room.

"Piper is missing, Arthur," Hoover said calmly. "She's a citizen of Jasper, but more importantly, a friend."

When the man did a dismissive shrug, it was all Shane could do not to jump out of his chair and show the man just how important. But before he could, Rutledge said, "Just remember our resources need to be used for all citizens, Hoover," and stepped from the room.

Ava laid a hand on his shoulder and applied gentle pressure there. "Ignore him, Shane," she said in a whisper only he could hear.

He shot her a look from the corner of his eye and didn't fail to see the compassion and determination there.

With a nod, he sat back and listened to the rest of the report and the plan to review various CCTV feeds from Jasper, just in case he had come through town, as well as some from the few cameras along the route in order to pinpoint where Parker might have gone with Piper.

"Chances are he went up into the mountains, so we'll have to round up some four-wheelers and get the chains on one of our police cruisers," Hoover instructed.

Brow furrowed, he glanced at Brady, who explained. "There's still snow at the higher elevations and with the thaw started, it'll be slush, but also icy in spots. You'll need to buy some chains for your pickup at the hardware store if you're coming with us."

"I'm coming with you."

PIPER WOKE TO the crack of splintering wood and a stream of foul language.

She slowly opened her eyes, her gaze unfocused as she searched the dim light in the cabin. Based on the shadows, she guessed that the sun was only just rising over the mountains. It had been pitch-dark the last time Josh had woken her to threaten harm if she didn't tell him where the relics were. He had done it several times during the course of the night, probably thinking the lack of sleep would loosen her tongue, not that she had anything to tell him.

The room was cold. So cold that her body was trembling in an effort to warm up.

The fire must have gone out during the night. No surprise since Josh had had little wood to feed it and keep it stoked.

Pieces of the chair in which he'd sat the night before lay before the hearth as Josh tried to get the fire going again. The bandanna he'd used to hold the gag in place was wrapped around his one hand and she assumed he'd injured himself.

He grabbed a few pieces of the chair and tossed them into the fireplace, but nothing happened.

"Match might help," she said. Her throat was dry, and her teeth chattered slightly as her body fought the cold.

"Shut up," he shouted over and over and advanced on her, fists clenched at his sides. It was cold enough for her to see his breath once he was nearly nose to nose with her.

She backed away as much as she could but winced at the pressure it put on her bound arms and hands that had been numb for hours. Her feet were numb now, too, from the cold, as was the tip of her nose.

"I'm cold," she said, but he only laughed, pulled away and wrapped the bandanna around his hand more tightly.

"Hurt yourself?" she asked, surprising herself with the real concern in her tone.

His brow furrowed as he peered at her and, sensing her sincerity, he said, "Ax broke when I tried to chop some more firewood. Handle splintered and cut me."

"You should see a doctor."

"I won't leave here until I get the answers I want from you," he said, but rubbed his hands against his arms, trying to get warm. Walking back and forth before her as she said again, "I'm cold."

"Tough. No matches, no fire," he said, dragging a harsh laugh from her.

"Not much of a Marine," she challenged, not caring if she angered him. Maybe if he got angry enough he'd do something stupid that might give her a chance to get free.

"Shut up," he shouted, then drew his palm across his short-cropped hair and grimaced since he'd used his injured hand.

"You should put a proper bandage on that. But of course, you don't have one, do you? Or an ax. Or matches or food from what I can see."

That pushed him to that edge, just like she hoped. He backhanded her across the face, rattling her teeth and sending the chair toppling backward. It landed with enough force to make her scream with agony at the weight it placed on her bound arms. Black circles danced around her gaze from the pain.

She screamed again and moaned as he grabbed the chair and set it upright. His features were tight, his face red with rage, lips drawn into a sneer.

"You better mind your mouth if you want to see tomorrow."

She waited for him to strike her once again, but instead he grabbed something from his back pocket. The rag he'd used as a gag the day before.

She dreaded the thought of it and he didn't miss seeing her fear.

"We can do this the easy way or the hard way. It's up to you."

SHANE HAD AGREED to meet Lieutenants Avery and Hoover at police headquarters once he'd gotten the chains for his pickup.

But he hadn't agreed to just sit around and do nothing after he'd left the meeting so the officers could do whatever other investigation was necessary before they headed up into the mountains.

Since their general consensus was that Parker had headed north in the general direction of the DCA, he'd packed up Decoy and gone back to where his pickup had been abandoned in the hopes that Decoy could locate some kind of scent. Unfortunately, although Decoy had sniffed around, he hadn't barked or done anything to alert him to a scent he recognized.

Although it had been dark, he'd driven around the areas near the DCA and beyond, but the roads had been fairly empty at that time of night. It had been nearly midnight when he'd driven back to Piper's house. The house seemed way too empty without Piper.

Even the dogs seemed to sense something was wrong as he leashed them and took them for a long walk, his mind racing with all the possibilities of where Piper might be. What might be happening to her.

His sleep had been troubled by those images and not even the presence of Decoy and Chipper had helped to soothe him. He'd risen before dawn and walked the dogs. Crated Chipper since he'd be gone most of the day. The puppy would feel secure in the comfortable crate.

Then he prepared, arming himself with conviction and something else: his Sig Sauer P320-M18. He also had a shotgun, but he could be more precise with the handgun if he needed to use it. Or least he hoped he could be precise.

Shane held the gun up and aimed it at a spot on the far wall of Piper's living room. His arm trembled as he did so, both from nerves and the sudden twitch of his injured shoulder muscles. It made his aim unsteady, so much so that he worried if it was more dangerous for him to be armed than not.

He hadn't held a gun in the many months since he'd left the Army. He didn't even know why he'd kept the weapon since he wasn't sure he could fire it with any accuracy. But maybe in the back of his mind he'd hoped that one day he could.

Maybe that day had come because he'd use every ounce of skill he had to make his shot true if it became necessary to use the gun to save Piper.

He loaded two magazines with 9mm bullets, slid a magazine into the pistol and chambered the first round.

He slipped the Sig Sauer into his holster, tucked the other magazine into his jacket pocket and was on his way out the door when he doubled back to Piper's bedroom to grab a dirty sweatshirt from her hamper.

It would have her scent on it and maybe Decoy would be able to track with that odor if Parker and she had gone on foot anywhere.

He quickly got Decoy into the pickup and rushed to the hardware store, intending to be ready to go with Jasper PD on their mountain search for Piper. There were already a few cars parked in front of the store and he hoped it wouldn't take long at the counter.

He got out of the car and took Decoy with him. Wrapping the leash around a bollard on the edge of the parking lot, he walked into the hardware store to look for the chains. He spotted them immediately at the end of a nearby counter and walked toward it.

A man hurried past him, struggling with two large bags. The man pushed through the door, but as he did so the side of one of the handles broke, making him drop the bag right by Decoy. A few items spilled out and he rushed to pick them up and stuff them back into the bag.

Meanwhile, Decoy sat up, stuck his nose out toward the man and started to bark, surprising the man, who rushed off. But Decoy kept on barking and glancing in the direction of the man, clearly agitated.

Shane rushed out of the store in time to see the man loading the bags into a white Jeep.

*White, not red like the Jeep that had been reported stolen in McCall*, he told himself, but something about the man and his actions was making his radar light up, especially since Decoy was still barking and straining at the leash.

In all his years in the military, he'd learned to trust that radar.

He untied the leash and got Decoy settled in the car, keeping an eye on the white Jeep all the time as it pulled out of the parking lot and turned onto the road. Hopping into his pickup, he quickly reversed and took off in the direction of the other vehicle, keeping a discreet distance. He couldn't fail to notice, however, that the four-wheeler was heading toward the mountains, right in the direction they had discussed the night before.

It was just too much coincidence, and if it was Parker he'd need backup, so he dialed Jasper PD.

Jenny the dispatcher answered and quickly patched him through to Brady. After he explained what had happened with Decoy, he said, "He's in a white Jeep, Brady. Not a red one."

Brady immediately answered. "I'll call McCall to confirm if a white Jeep was also reported stolen. Are you still following it?"

"I am. I can send you my location to track with my phone," Shane said.

"Do that. Ava and I will catch up to you," Brady said and hung up.

Shane fumbled with his phone to send Brady the text message with the tracking to his location. He had slowed while doing that, increasing the distance between him and the Jeep. So far nothing the driver had done indicated that he thought he was being followed. But as the car pulled off onto a side road and stopped, as if to see if he would follow, he drove past, hoping that the side road only led one way: to Piper.

He didn't know why, but he was sure now that the man in the Jeep was Parker. Especially as he recalled how the man had looked, with a baseball cap pulled low and jacket collar turned up, as if to hide his features.

Which meant he had to follow Parker up the mountain.

Executing a K-turn, he headed back quickly to the side road, slowing as he neared it. In the early morning light, the Jeep's taillights were visible along the side road, halfway up the mountain.

Shane shut off his lights, turned onto the side road and hurried after Parker.

Piper had been dozing, trying to make up for the night of Josh's constant interruptions, when she heard a car pull up.

Josh. She didn't know how long she'd been asleep, but it didn't feel like long. She peered through the dirty glass and plastic on the windows. A white Jeep had pulled up, Josh at the wheel. The sun was still low on the horizon, hinting at the fact that he hadn't been gone long, maybe an hour or so.

That told her that wherever they were wasn't all that far from Jasper. If she could get free and make it down the mountain, she might be able to flag someone on the road to take her to town.

She shifted in the seat again as she had been doing all night, trying to restore feeling to her hands and feet with little luck. They were still numb.

Barely a minute later, Josh pushed through the door,

carrying two bags. He walked to a small table at one side of the room and took out supplies: an ax, matches, a first aid kit and a few cans of food.

He fumbled with the first aid kit, opening it and cursing as he wiped his cut with an alcohol pad. Then he wrapped gauze around his hand, pushed the kit aside and picked up the ax. Sunlight glinted off the shiny metal as he ran a finger across the edge, testing its sharpness.

With a nod, he walked toward her, and it was clear that he had no intention of using the ax to cut firewood.

WITHOUT THE CHAINS Shane hadn't been able to buy at the hardware store, he hadn't made it past the first half a mile or so of slushy snow at the higher elevations. The car had slipped and slid until he'd lost control and almost hit a tree by the side of the road. He'd also worried that the sound of the engine would carry up the mountain and alert Parker that he had been discovered.

He needed the element of surprise if he was going to overpower Parker and save Piper.

Tucking his cell phone into his pocket so Jasper PD could keep on tracking him, he opened the door for Decoy and slipped off his leash. He grabbed Piper's dirty sweatshirt and let Decoy smell it, hoping he'd pick up Piper's scent to help guide him in case the road ahead didn't lead straight to Parker.

Together, Decoy and he trudged up through the slush, snow and patches of ice where the snow had melted and refrozen overnight. It was slow going, his feet slipping beneath him regularly, but he pushed on, aware that time wasn't on his side.

Parker had taken Piper in the late afternoon and had her overnight. He'd want her to tell him where she had the relics her husband had supposedly sent her, but he was as sure as Piper that Lambert wasn't the one who had taken them. That left one person who might have them: Buck Devare.

Unfortunately, Parker's good friend Buck had probably convinced him that he didn't have the relics. Shane wasn't as convinced.

He had gone about a mile up the road when he spotted something white through a thicket of trees. Looking more closely, he realized the road took a big bend to the left and that it was the white Jeep Parker had been driving, parked in front of a cabin that was in pretty bad shape. Broken windows, taped over with plastic. Missing planks of wood on the front porch and a gaping hole in one corner of a roof that looked ready to collapse.

He rushed up the last part of the road, careful not to make too much sound. Signaling to Decoy to stay close and quiet.

Decoy glanced at him and seemed to nod in understanding.

Creeping up the last few feet, hunched over to hopefully avoid being seen through the windows, he managed to get on the front porch noiselessly. Crouching low, he peered through the window.

Piper was duct-taped to a chair and Parker was circling her, an ax in his hand and a gun in a holster on his hip.

"You've been trying my patience all night and I'm done waiting. Next time I get an 'I don't know,' it'll cost you a toe or two," he said, slapping the ax handle in his hand over and over.

Shane couldn't delay as hundreds of scenarios raced through his brain.

The ax slicing through the air, catching Piper on the shoulder. The neck. Her lifeblood seeping from her as he stood there, waiting for the right moment to attack.

He slipped his Sig Sauer from the holster, hand trembling as he did so, but from fear. More fear than he'd ever experienced on any mission when he'd been in the Army because this time the woman he loved was in danger.

He couldn't deny it any longer: he loved Piper.

Tightening his hand on the grip, he crept to the door, grabbed the handle and threw the door open.

It bounced against the wall with a noisy thud, snagging Parker's attention.

He raised the ax and Shane issued one command to Decoy. He hoped that this time the dog wouldn't hesitate.

"Attack."

Decoy leaped at Parker, latching onto his biceps and driving him away from Piper and onto the ground with the force of his leap.

Shane rushed forward, snatched the ax from Parker and threw it across the room as the other man fought to get Decoy off him, rolling from side to side, but Decoy hung on.

Shane pinned Parker's other arm to the ground with his knee, then took the gun from Parker's hip holster and tossed it aside, well out of Parker's reach.

"Stop," he commanded, and Decoy immediately released Parker's arm.

Parker swung his now-free hand up, trying to cuff Shane across the side of the head, but Shane blocked the blow with his left arm. He punched Parker with the hand that still held the gun, dazing him.

Rolling Parker onto his stomach, he placed a knee in the middle of his back and pointed his gun at Parker's head.

"Don't move, Parker."

"She's got the relics. Don't let her kid you about that," Parker said, his voice bordering on crazy.

"She doesn't have anything, Parker," he said and looked around for something he could use to bind Parker's arms, but just then, the crunch of tires on ice and snow and a car engine told him the cavalry had arrived.

Ava and Brady rushed through the door, guns drawn, but they quickly holstered them as they realized Shane had Parker under control.

Ava immediately went to Piper to cut away the duct tape, while Brady came over to handcuff Parker and haul him to his feet.

Shane rushed to Piper's side, knelt by her and cupped her cheek. There was an ugly bruise near her temple and an angry splotch of red on her cheek. "Are you okay?"

Piper nodded but grimaced with pain as she finally moved her unbound arms. At his questioning glance, she said, "He hit me with the gun butt but right now it's a lot of pins and needles. Sore. He bounced me around in the chair and I landed on my arms."

He stroked his hand along her forearm and down to

twine his fingers with hers. "Let's get you to the hospital where they can check you out."

"I'm okay. I'd rather go home," she said as she rubbed her wrists.

Shane shook his head. "We're not going to take any chances. Hospital and then we can head home and get you into a hot bath. It'll help the aches."

She offered up a little smile and reluctantly nodded. "Hospital. Home. Together. That sounds like a great idea."

## *Chapter Twenty-Two*

Piper lazed in the hot water of the bath that Shane had graciously drawn when they had first gotten home.

Home. It hadn't felt like home when she had first come here from California, but little by little the area, dogs and people had worked themselves into her heart. But somehow deep inside she had sensed something else was missing.

But not anymore.

She swiped some errant soap bubbles from her arms and noticed the bruises on her biceps and wrists from being banged around and tied up. She ran a hand across one particularly larger bruise and winced. It was tender to the touch.

The water in the bath slowly grew tepid, her fingers wrinkly, warning Piper that it was time to get out.

Easing from the tub, she toweled down and slipped on a robe, grimacing as soreness awoke in another spot high up on her shoulder.

It would take days for all the aches to fade away, but there was another pain that would linger far longer. The pain of Shane leaving.

Their lessons were as good as over. Both Shane and

Decoy were ready to go to the search and rescue group in Montana to continue their training. And now that the danger from Josh Parker was over, there was nothing keeping Shane in Jasper any longer.

Her heart clenched at the thought, felt like it was breaking into hundreds of pieces, but she belted the robe tight around her, as if that would keep the pieces from falling out of her chest.

As she walked out of the bathroom and into her bedroom, the smells of coffee, bacon and eggs snared her attention.

Hurrying forward, she caught sight of Shane at the stove, cooking. He turned and smiled as he saw her.

"Feeling better?" he said and raised the pan to tip out scrambled eggs onto two plates sitting on the counter.

She nodded. "Much. Thank you for everything."

He picked up the plates and sauntered over to the dining table near the sliding doors. Set them down and waited for her to take a seat at the table, his hands clenching awkwardly on the top rung of a nearby chair. Waiting for her to sit, ever the gentleman, although she sensed his hesitation was about more than just manners.

She sat and he finally took a chair opposite hers, his movements tentative as he reached for one of the coffee cups on the table. He filled it from a carafe and handed it to her.

Her hands trembled as she took the cup, added cream and sugar, and stirred, over and over, the spoon rattling noisily against the cup until Shane reached over and gentled her with his touch.

"It's going to be okay," he said, almost as if this nightmare wasn't over.

Narrowing her gaze to gauge his answer, she said, "What aren't you telling me?"

His lips thinned into a tight line, and he drew his hand away. She felt immediately bereft.

"Parker is insisting your husband took the relics." He picked up his coffee cup and took a bracing sip, wincing at the heat of it.

"David was an honest man. He would never have stolen anything." She grabbed her cup and cradled it between her hands, hoping the heat of the mug would help chase away the sudden chill in her heart.

"My friend had told me that the Marines didn't believe David had taken anything. He had reported the relics, which makes no sense if he intended to steal them."

"But?" she said, hearing what he wasn't saying.

"Parker's actions have forced the authorities to reopen the investigations. Since we're sure there's nothing here, they're going to visit Buck Devare."

"Josh's partner. The other man who received the dishonorable discharge," she said and finally lifted her cup to take a sip.

"Yes. They're going there today," he said and motioned to her dish. "Eat up before it gets cold."

She did, forking up some of the eggs and a slice of the bacon. She hadn't really felt hungry at first, especially with the earlier discussion, but after the first few bites, hunger kicked in, and in no time she had finished all the eggs and bacon and a few slices of buttered toast.

"That was delicious," she said and rose to pick up the plates, but Shane laid a hand on hers to stop her.

"I'll clean up. You should try and get some rest. You had a rough night," he said and again she heard what he wasn't saying: it might turn out to be a rough day as well.

She rose slowly, more aches and pains announcing their presence. As he headed to the kitchen sink with the plates, she went back to her bedroom, feeling the weight of the night before dragging her down. Closing the door, she slipped off her robe and slid beneath the sheets. They were cool against her body, but warmth soon built in the cocoon around her and the comfort of it and lack of sleep from the night before pulled her into unconsciousness.

SHANE HEARD HER bedroom door closing and laid his wet hands on the edge of the counter. Drawing in a long breath, he fought the urge to go comfort her.

She'd been through hell the day before, but he worried that whatever the authorities discovered after their visit to Devare would plunge her into an even worse hell.

His cell phone rang, and he dried his hands and checked the caller ID. Emma. He swiped to answer.

"How's she doing?" Emma immediately asked.

"She's…tired. Banged up." He had seen the bruises and abrasions on her wrists as she'd held the coffee cup.

"How did she handle the news about the investigation?" Emma said, worry alive in her voice.

"Badly, I think. She defended her husband—"

"She loved him with all her heart, and he was a good guy, Shane. I met him several times and I can't imagine him ever doing something like that," Emma said, clearly as loyal to Lambert as Piper. Even though he hadn't known him, if two women like Piper and Emma spoke for him, he must have been a good man.

"I know, but we need to let the investigation play out," he said, urging a patience he wasn't feeling. He wanted the investigation to be over sooner rather than later so that Piper could get on with her life.

"I got a call yesterday from the search and rescue group in Montana. With everything going on, I didn't get a chance to tell you. They were asking for a recommendation from the DCA for you."

A recommendation from Emma would help him continue with his training, only…

"Thanks. I'd appreciate that," he said.

"Great," she said, but her tone was ambiguous as if she didn't really believe he intended to go through with it.

"I'll keep you posted on what's happening," he said and swiped to end the call.

SINCE THE INCIDENT with Parker a few days earlier, Piper and Shane distracted themselves by working with Decoy and Chipper on the agility course. Decoy had mastered the basic obstacles as well as the more complicated chutes and tunnels they'd added. Chipper had proved herself adept despite her shorter legs.

"Maybe I'll train her for the agility course competitions," Piper said with a laugh as Chipper sped over the A frame and into the tunnel.

"She's fast," Shane said and shook his head at the little dog's antics.

But as Chipper finished the course and raced right at Decoy to play with her best friend, Piper noticed the

Jasper PD cruiser parking across from Emma's ranch house.

Emma must have noticed it as well since she came out of the DCA offices and walked to join Shane and her at the training ring fence.

Ava and Brady exited the cruiser and walked over, their body postures easygoing and smiles on their faces.

"I guess you have good news," Shane said and laid a hand at the small of her back, offering support even though she didn't think she'd need it.

"We do. The authorities visited Buck Devare. At first, he denied everything, but little by little they wore him down. He admitted that he had taken the relics after your husband had reported their discovery, but before he and Parker went back to get them," Ava reported, and relief filled Piper that her husband's memory would be clear of any stain on his character.

"How did he get them out of Iraq?" Shane asked.

"They were small carved tablets and cylindrical stamps as well as a gold bracelet from Sumer. He hid them in his uniform pockets since he hoped he wouldn't be searched. Once he got home, he found an antiquities dealer who wasn't very concerned about their provenance," Brady added to the report.

"What happens now?" Emma asked and shot a relieved glance in Piper's direction.

"Devare will likely cop a deal in exchange for the name of the dealer. Apparently the last time something like this happened, the relic thief got eighteen months' probation and had to make restitution to the dealer," Ava advised.

Piper raised an eyebrow. "That's all? After everything that's happened?"

Ava and Brady shared a look that communicated they were as frustrated as Piper with the sentence. "At least Parker's going to get more. Burglary. Assault and battery. Kidnapping. He's going to spend a long time behind bars," Brady said.

"And the antiquities dealer?" Shane asked.

"They paid him a visit and got the relics back. He hadn't been able to sell them without the provenance. They'll be returned to the Iraqi authorities," Ava advised.

"So it's over," Piper said and suddenly her knees were sagging.

Shane's arm was quickly around her waist, drawing her close to offer support.

"You and Shane may have to testify at Parker's trial, but other than that, it's over. You're safe," Ava said and laid a compassionate hand on Piper's arm.

"Thank you both," she said, forcing a smile to allay the officers' fears about her well-being.

Shane echoed her sentiment. "We appreciate all you did to help catch Parker."

Brady did a little shrug. "We owe a big thanks to your quick thinking and Decoy over there," he said and jerked his head in the direction of where the two dogs were playfully chasing each other around the training ring. "You and he are going to make a fine addition to any search and rescue group."

Piper couldn't miss the way Shane's body tensed against hers with the SAR mention. They hadn't talked about it in the last few days, but both of them knew it was there, festering like a wound.

Ava's radio chirped, alerting them that they were needed. "Unit 12. We've got a 10-46 on East Crabapple about a mile from the Salmon River," Jenny said over the radio.

"On it," Ava confirmed. With a smile, she explained, "Motorist needs some help."

"We'll see you soon," Brady advised and with a wave, the two of them were off to their cruiser.

"I guess I should get back to work," Emma said and, after hugging both of them, headed toward the DCA offices.

Piper watched Emma walk away, and in her ear Shane said, "Relax. It really is all going to be okay."

Only it wasn't going to be all right and it was long past time to discuss it.

She turned in Shane's arms, but he didn't release her, bringing his hands to her waist as she looked up at him.

"Now that it's over, you'll be going soon. You and Decoy are more than ready to continue your training with that Montana SAR group. Chipper is going to miss him," she said and glanced toward the dogs, who were still happily playing together.

SHANE COULDN'T CONTAIN the laugh that escaped him. With a shake of his head, he said, "Is Chipper the only one who's going to be missing someone?"

Bright color erupted across her cheeks, and she looked away, avoiding his gaze.

He cupped her cheek, applied gentle pressure to have

her face him and stroked a finger across her creamy skin. "You know I'm going to miss you, Shane."

"I'd miss you, too, Piper, because…I love you."

Her gaze widened and her mouth formed a surprised *O*. "You love me?"

He grinned and shook his head lightheartedly. "I love you and I hope you feel the same."

She answered him by rising up on tiptoes and kissing him. He could feel the smile on her lips, and warmth filled his heart with her joy.

He wrapped his arms around her waist and brought her near, her softness fitting perfectly against him as the kiss deepened. His body responded, hardening with the feel of her, bringing a reminder of where they were and that he had something else to say to her.

Tempering the kiss, he sucked in a shaky breath, and she did the same, but then she said, "I love you, but… You're going to Montana."

He once again cradled her cheek and said, "After the other night, I realized I couldn't leave you… I mean, that is if you don't want me to go."

"I don't want you to go," she said with a broad smile. Her green eyes glittered like emeralds in the bright sun.

Grinning, he said, "I'm glad because I spoke to Gonzo and he suggested someone who can help me with the nightmares and PTSD. Then I called the local SAR group. They'd love to have Decoy and me train with them. That is if you'll have me. Permanently."

She arched a brow and her gaze skittered across his face. "Permanently?"

He nodded. "Yes, as in, I want to marry you, Piper

Lambert. Train dogs together. Maybe have some kids if you want."

"I want. Really, really want. I love you, Shane Adler. I want to train dogs with you and yes, I would like to have kids someday," she said, laughter in her voice as she laid her hands on his shoulders and kissed him.

Shane joined in her laughter and her kiss, certain that he was meant to be with Piper here in Jasper. Meant to live in these mountains that had brought him so much peace and this woman who had made that peace complete.

A bump against his leg reluctantly broke them apart.

Chipper and Decoy sat at their feet, looking up at them. Chipper had that irrepressible grin on her face while Decoy's head was tilted at a questioning angle until he said, "We're home, Decoy. We're finally home."

"I like the sound of that. How about you, Chipper?" Piper said and the little dog barked.

"I guess that's a yes," Shane said, grinning.

"Definitely a yes. What do you say about us going home to celebrate?" Piper said.

Home. It sounded so nice on her lips and his as he said, "Let's go home."

\* \* \* \* \*

*The K-9s on Patrol series continues next month with*
Sniffing Out Danger *by Elizabeth Heiter.*
*You'll find it wherever*
*Harlequin Intrigue books are sold!*

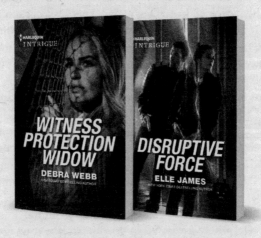

## #2067 SNIFFING OUT DANGER
*K-9s on Patrol* • by Elizabeth Heiter

When former big-city cop Ava Callan stumbles upon a bomb, she seizes the chance to prove herself to the small-town police department where she's becoming a K-9 handler...but especially to charming lead investigator Eli Thorne. The only thing more explosive than her chemistry with the out-of-town captain? The danger menacing them at every turn...

## #2068 UNDERCOVER COUPLE
*A Ree and Quint Novel* • by Barb Han

Legendary ATF agent Quint Casey isn't thrilled to pose as Ree Sheppard's husband for a covert investigation into a weapons ring that could be tied to his past. But when his impetuous "wife" proves her commitment to the job, Quint feels a spark just as alarming as the dangerous killers he's sworn to unmask.

## #2069 DODGING BULLETS IN BLUE VALLEY
*A North Star Novel Series* • by Nicole Helm

When the attempted rescue of his infant twins goes horribly wrong, Blue Valley sheriff Garret Averly and North Star doctor Betty Wagner take the mission into their own hands. Deep in the Montana mountains and caught in a deadly storm, he's willing to sacrifice everything to bring Betty and his children home safely.

## #2070 TO CATCH A KILLER
*Heartland Heroes* • by Julie Anne Lindsey

Apprehending a violent fugitive is US marshal Nash Winchester's top priority when Great Falls chef Lana Iona becomes the next target as the sole eyewitness to a murder. Forced to stay constantly on the move, can the Kentucky lawman stop a killer from permanently silencing the woman he's never forgotten?

## #2071 ACCIDENTAL AMNESIA
*The Saving Kelby Creek Series* • by Tyler Anne Snell

Awakening in an ambulance headed to Kelby Creek, Melanie Blankenship can't remember why or how she got there. While she's back in the town that turned on her following her ex-husband's shocking scandal, evidence mounts against Mel in a deadly crime. Can her former love Deputy Sterling Costner uncover the criminal before she pays the ultimate price?

## #2072 THE BODY IN THE WALL
*A Badge of Courage Novel* • by Rita Herron

The sooner Special Agent Macy Stark can sell her childhood home, the sooner she can escape her small town and shameful past—until she discovers a body in the wall and her childhood nightmares return. Handsome local sheriff Stone Lawson joins the cold case—but someone will stop at nothing to keep the past hidden.

## SPECIAL EXCERPT FROM

**HQN**

*Sheriff Matt Corbin never expected to return to his hometown of Last Ridge, Texas. Nor did he ever imagine he'd be reunited with his childhood crush, Emory Parkman, a successful wedding-dress designer who's been even unluckier in love than Matt. And yet there she is, living on the family ranch he now owns... and working just as hard as he is to fight the attraction that's only getting stronger by the day...*

*Read on for a sneak peek of*
Summer at Stallion Ridge,
*part of the Last Ride, Texas, series*
*from USA TODAY bestselling author Delores Fossen.*

"I wouldn't have bought the place if I'd known you would ever come back here to live," she explained. "You always said you'd get out and stay out, come hell or high water."

Yeah, he'd indeed said that all right. Now he was eating those words. "Anything else going on with you that I should know about?"

"I'm making Natalie's wedding dress," she readily admitted.

Maybe she thought she'd see some disapproval on his face over that. She wouldn't. Matt didn't necessarily buy into the bunk about Emory's dresses being *mostly lucky*, but he wanted Natalie to be happy. Because that in turn would improve Jack's chances of being happy. If Vince Parkman and Last Ride were what Natalie needed for that happiness, then Matt was willing to give the man, and the town, his blessing.

"Anything else?" he pressed. "I'd like not to get blindsided by something else for at least the next twenty-four hours."

Emory cocked her head to the side, studying him again.

Then smiling. Not a big beaming smile but one with a sly edge to it. "You mean like nightly loud parties, nude gardening or weddings in the pasture?"

Of course, his brain, and another stupid part of him, latched right on to the nude gardening. The breeze didn't help, either, because it swirled her dress around again, this time lifting it up enough for him to get a glimpse of her thigh.

Her smile widened. "No loud parties, weddings in the pasture and I'll keep nude gardening to a minimum." She stuck out her hand. "Want to shake on that?"

Matt was sure he was frowning, but it had nothing to do with the truce she obviously wanted. It was because he was trying to figure out how the hell he was going to look out the kitchen window and not get a too-clear image of Emory naked except for gardening gloves.

He shook his head, but because the stupid part of him was still playing into this, his gaze locked on her mouth. That mouth he suddenly wanted to taste.

"The last time I kissed you, your brothers saw it and beat me up. Repeatedly," he grumbled.

No way had he intended to say that aloud. It'd just popped out. Of course, no way had he wanted to have the urge to kiss Emory, either.

"It's not a good idea for us to be living so close to each other," Matt managed to add.

"Don't worry," she said, her voice a sexy siren's purr. "You'll never even notice I'm here." With a smile that was the perfect complement to that purr, she fluttered her fingers in a little wave, turned and walked toward the cottage.

Matt just stood there, knowing that what she'd said was a Texas-sized lie. Oh, yeah, he would notice all right.

*Don't miss*
**Summer at Stallion Ridge**
*by Delores Fossen, available April 2022 wherever HQN books and ebooks are sold.*

**HQNBooks.com**

PHDFEXP0322

# Get 4 FREE REWARDS!

**We'll send you 2 FREE Books <u>plus</u> 2 FREE Mystery Gifts.**

KENTUCKY CRIME RING
JULIE ANNE LINDSEY

TEXAS STALKER
BARB HAN

**FREE** Value Over **$20**

UNDER THE RANCHER'S PROTECTION
ADDISON FOX

OPERATION WHISTLEBLOWER
JUSTINE DAVIS

Both the **Harlequin Intrigue®** and **Harlequin® Romantic Suspense** series feature compelling novels filled with heart-racing action-packed romance that will keep you on the edge of your seat.

---

**YES!** Please send me 2 FREE novels from the Harlequin Intrigue or Harlequin Romantic Suspense series and my 2 FREE gifts (gifts are worth about $10 retail). After receiving them, if I don't wish to receive any more books, I can return the shipping statement marked "cancel." If I don't cancel, I will receive 6 brand-new Harlequin Intrigue Larger-Print books every month and be billed just $5.99 each in the U.S. or $6.49 each in Canada, a savings of at least 14% off the cover price or 4 brand-new Harlequin Romantic Suspense books every month and be billed just $4.99 each in the U.S. or $5.74 each in Canada, a savings of at least 13% off the cover price. It's quite a bargain! Shipping and handling is just 50¢ per book in the U.S. and $1.25 per book in Canada.* I understand that accepting the 2 free books and gifts places me under no obligation to buy anything. I can always return a shipment and cancel at any time. The free books and gifts are mine to keep no matter what I decide.

Choose one: ☐ **Harlequin Intrigue Larger-Print** (199/399 HDN GNXC)  ☐ **Harlequin Romantic Suspense** (240/340 HDN GNMZ)

Name (please print)

Address                                                                      Apt. #

City                              State/Province                    Zip/Postal Code

Email: Please check this box ☐ if you would like to receive newsletters and promotional emails from Harlequin Enterprises ULC and its affiliates. You can unsubscribe anytime.

**Mail to the Harlequin Reader Service:**
**IN U.S.A.: P.O. Box 1341, Buffalo, NY 14240-8531**
**IN CANADA: P.O. Box 603, Fort Erie, Ontario L2A 5X3**

**Want to try 2 free books from another series! Call 1-800-873-8635 or visit www.ReaderService.com.**

---

HIHRS22

Five years of memories didn't compare an ounce to the man
they'd been made about. Not when he seemingly materialized
out of midair, wrapped in a uniform that fit nicely, topped
with a cowboy hat his daddy had given him and carrying
some emotions behind clear blue eyes.

Eyes that, once they found Mel during her attempt to flee
the hospital, never strayed.

Not that she'd expected anything but full attention when
Sterling Costner found out she was back in town.

Though, silly ol' Mel had been hoping that she'd have more
time before she had this face-to-face.

Because, as much as she was hoping no one else would
catch wind of her arrival, she knew the gossip mill around
town was probably already aflame.

"I'm glad this wasn't destroyed," Mel said lamely once
she slid into the passenger seat, picking up her suitcase in the
process. She placed it on her lap.

She remembered leaving her apartment with it, but not
what she'd packed inside. At least now she could change out
of her hospital gown.

Sterling slid into his truck like a knife through butter.

The man could make anything look good.

"I didn't see your car, but Deputy Rossi said it looked like someone hit your back end," he said once the door was shut. "Whoever hit you probably got spooked and took off. We're looking for them, though, so don't worry."

Mel's stomach moved a little at that last part.

"Don't worry" in Sterling's voice used to be the soundtrack to her life. A comforting repetition that felt like it could fix everything.

She played with the zipper on her suitcase.

"I guess I'll deal with the technical stuff tomorrow. Not sure what my insurance is going to say about the whole situation. I suppose it depends on how many cases of amnesia they get."

Sterling shrugged. He was such a big man that even the most subtle movements drew attention.

"I'm sure you'll do fine with them," he said.

She decided talking about her past was as bad as talking about theirs, so she looked out the window and tried to pretend for a moment that nothing had changed.

That she hadn't married Rider Partridge.

That she hadn't waited so long to divorce him.

That she hadn't fallen in love with Sterling.

That she hadn't—

Mel sat up straighter.

She glanced at Sterling and found him already looking at her.

She smiled.

It wasn't returned.

*Don't miss*
Accidental Amnesia *by Tyler Anne Snell,*
*available May 2022 wherever*
*Harlequin Intrigue books and ebooks are sold.*

Harlequin.com